WASHOE COUNTY LIBR.

P9-AFI-915

3 1235 03633 8080

What people are saying about *The Cage,*
First Book in the Birthright Series:

Great book! Couldn't put it down!

I blew through this book and can't wait to read the rest of the series! It wasn't predictable and the story and characters kept me hooked!

—*Sarah Monahan*

Great characters & story

The teenage characters in this book came alive with their issues and problems. I really cared for them and wanted them to succeed in both their personal growth as well as solving the problem that the dreams presented. I am glad this will be a series because I am anxious to learn more about them and what happens to them. Great read!

—*Less Flynn*

Relevant and Refreshing!

I found this book relevant and refreshing! Not only does this book touch on a relevant topic of sex trafficking in an engaging way, but the author presents characters that are real....so real that I could see a little bit of myself in each character. I especially loved the fact that the author also brought up the topic of the "art of listening". This is also another issue that I realize we don't do well in our culture. Not only did I enjoy the story line immensely, but I felt challenged to listen well to others.

— *Amy Hauptman*

A Great read!

Mystery, relationships, adventure, and spirituality--what a great combination. This is a quick read and very engaging. The author shows a lot of insight into issues teens face: the struggles, challenges and hopes. It was easy to identify with the characters. The plot was pretty fascinating as the author combines day-to-day relationship issues with this rather unique, unnerving dilemma and a touch of the transcendent. While the mystery is solved, the transcendent/spiritual aspect is left pleasantly and ambiguously unresolved. A good book for teens and people who care about them.

—*Paul Sorrentino*

Great Read

Read this book right away and found it intriguing, entertaining and informative. I highly recommend it to anyone but especially young people of any age.

—*Barbara Brown*

Powerful

I could hardly put this book down! The Cage captured my attention immediately and held it tight all the way to the end. Jacci Turner uses the medium of young adult fiction to skillfully and inadvertently teach about personalities, group dynamics, current social tragedies, and spiritual realities. Turner has a gift for explaining the supernatural in an understandable way by smoothly weaving explanation into her storyline. Turner also stirs the reader's heart to action as she grippingly exposes one of the most horrific tragedies of our day. I definitely recommend this book!

—*Katie May*

The Bar

Second Book of The Birthright Series

by

Jacci Turner

Lucky Bat Books

The Bar
Second Book in The Birthright Series
Copyright 2012, Jacci Turner
Cover Artist Chris Heifner, Copyright 2012

All rights reserved.

Published by
Lucky Bat Books
LuckyBatBooks.com
10 9 8 7 6 5 4 3 2 1

DEDICATION

For my daughter, Sarah (my Boo), you know my books couldn't exist without your love, help and support. This one comes with fond memories of road trips and trespassing, like most of our adventures. You are my hero and I want to be like you when I grow up!   *~Mom*

CHAPTER THIRTEEN
Emily 70

CHAPTER FOURTEEN
Sammy 75

CHAPTER FIFTEEN
Brandi 81

CHAPTER SIXTEEN
Teddy 90

CHAPTER SEVENTEEN
Emily 94

CHAPTER EIGHTEEN
Sammy 97

CHAPTER NINETEEN
Emily 100

CHAPTER TWENTY
Sammy 108

CHAPTER TWENTY-ONE
Emily 111

CHAPTER TWENTY-TWO
Sammy 124

EPILOGUE
The Rally 128

ACKNOWLEDGEMENTS

DEAR READER

CONTENTS

DEDICATION

CHAPTER ONE
Emily   1

CHAPTER TWO
Emily   6

CHAPTER THREE
Emily   10

CHAPTER FOUR
Brandi   17

CHAPTER FIVE
Emily   20

CHAPTER SIX
Emily   25

CHAPTER SEVEN
Sammy   29

CHAPTER EIGHT
Emily   37

CHAPTER NINE
Dawna   45

CHAPTER TEN
Emily   49

CHAPTER ELEVEN
Dawna   55

CHAPTER TWELVE
Teddy   64

The Bar

Second Book of The Birthright Series

by

Jacci Turner

CHAPTER ONE
EMILY

IT WAS DURING LUNCH ON MONDAY that Emily's anger blew a gasket. They had to eat lunch at the nearby elementary school because her small high school had no lunchroom. She was sitting at the table of freshman girls who ate together more out of survival than affinity. Even though most of these students had been in classes together since kindergarten, the freshmen still got treated like second class citizens at Loyalton High.

Big-mouthed Candace brought up the approaching trial of Emily's big sister Dawna. Of course everyone was talking about it. It was the biggest event their small town had seen since the gold rush. But Emily thought it was rude of Candace to bring the trial up in front of her. Any moron could see how worried Emily and her family were. She shot Candace a death glare, but Candace went on without taking a breath.

"Oh, and did you hear? All the kidnapped girls will be filmed when they testify. Of course they'll blur out their faces, and change their voices, but we'll know which one Dawna is."

Emily's temper boiled over and she stood up shouting, "Shut up Candace! Just shut up!"

The whole table of girls stared at her in shocked silence. Kids at tables nearby stopped talking and turned to stare. Her face was hot with embarrassment. She threw her half-eaten baloney sandwich into the garbage as she ran out the front door.

The September wind flowing down from the Sierra Nevada mountain range whipped her face as she jogged the football-length strip of grass back to the high school. Mad enough to kick herself, she couldn't believe she'd let them get to her! Her carefully built wall of protection was threatening to crumble.

Her older sister Dawna had run away last summer. She had been sick of living in the tiny town of Sierraville and had hitchhiked away with dreams of becoming a model. After a couple of days of hunger and sleeping on the streets of Sacramento, she was taken by men targeting runaways and selling them for sex to truck drivers. Dawna was lucky. She managed to escape before being raped and was returned in a rather mysterious fashion by a car full of teenagers. Now the trial of the sex traffickers was beginning and Dawna's parents moved her an hour away to her aunt and uncle in Reno, Nevada to escape the small town gossip. But Emily could not escape it. She and her family heard the whispers and sly digs daily—*she deserved it.*

She flung open the front door of the high school and ran into the girl's bathroom. The sound of her feet echoed off the tile floor, and the smell of cleaning fluid assaulted her nose. Suddenly, disoriented by what she saw, she reached for the wall to steady herself. It was not that she didn't know who she was looking at, that part was easy. Brandi Burges was one of the most recognizable girls in her entire high school. Her mix of Chinese and Caucasian blood made her beauty exotic. Her upbeat temperament made her a shoo-in for head cheerleader, and her scholastic ability made her top candidate for this year's valedictorian. What confused Emily was what to do. She saw Brandi lying against the back wall of the restroom in her cheerleading outfit, curled into a tight ball. Brandi's eyes were wide with fear. She was making a small whimpering sound as her chest heaved, gasping to breathe.

Normally, Emily would have walked forward without hesitation to offer assistance. But seeing Brandi Burges like this was not even in the realm of normal.

Emily looked around the room frantically searching for a hidden camera. Or maybe there were some girls, hiding in a stall, waiting to laugh at the freshman who had fallen for their prank. She found no camera, and the stalls and small room were empty. Brandi stayed on the floor, her eyes trained on Emily. Slowly, Emily approached, bending toward her and asked in a quiet voice: "Are you okay?"

Brandi gave her head the slightest shake. Emily began to panic. Should she run out to get help, or stay here and try to help Brandi herself? Brandi's eyes made the decision for Emily. She had seen this haunted look before. When Dawna came back home in the middle of the night last summer — her eyes had this same caged animal look. Emily got down on the floor next to Brandi, and gently put her hand on Brandi's arm.

"You're going be all right," she whispered.

Brandi seemed to calm at Emily's touch. Emily reached over her and gently grabbed Brandi's shoulders, and lifted her into a sitting position. She smelled perfume, the same kind Dawna used, made by

Britney Spears. They sat side-by-side on the bathroom floor while Brandi's breathing slowed, and her body relaxed. Emily kept stroking her arm repeating softly, "You'll be all right."

"Can you help me get up?" Brandi asked with a shaky voice.

Emily stood and grasped Brandi's hands, slowly pulling the much taller girl to her feet. Brandi leaned against Emily for support.

"Would you like help to the office?"

Brandi nodded, and they took a faltering step forward. Just then the door flew open and a crowd of cheerleaders entered the bathroom in a hailstorm of laughter. One look at Brandi's deathly white face and the loud chatter stopped. Suddenly, overlapping concerned voices echoed off the bathroom walls.

"Brandi, are you okay?"

"What happened?"

"Should I call 911?"

Brandi looked down at the floor then flicked a warning glance at Emily,

"I think I fainted," she said in a whisper. "Can you take me to the nurse?"

Brandi's posse swept in like soldiers on a rescue mission. They pushed Emily out of the way and quickly marched Brandi out of the bathroom.

Emily stood alone in the room, unsure what to think about what she'd just witnessed. She muttered, "She didn't faint, but what happened to her?"

The fact that she was summarily dismissed by Brandi's friends didn't bother her. The social order of high school was so prescribed

Emily had no illusions she should be noticed by such a popular group of upperclassman. *But why did Brandi lie? What was she covering up?*

Emily thought about this for another minute, and then had a happy revelation. It may have been her first happy thought of the whole day. *At least the school will have something new to talk about!* A small school was like a small town. Word of Brandi's "fainting spell" would be spreading like wildfire already and attention would be turned away from the approaching trial. Emily left the bathroom, smiling.

CHAPTER TWO
EMILY

WEDNESDAY, JUST AS EMILY was leaving her last class to catch the school bus, she remembered her homework. She forgot the art piece she was working on in her class, and she ran back in to get it. It was due Friday, and she needed to work on it tonight in order to finish it on time. Just outside the art class door she heard voices and stopped. Two teachers were talking in low tones near the door.

The first voice was Mr. Miles, the math teacher and football coach. He was the dad of John and Joe Miles who were both on the football team. Most of the teachers had other jobs at her small school, and parent volunteers ran all of the sports programs. His voice was low, "They don't know what happened but her parents had to go pick her up at the practice last night. She was practically comatose!"

"Poor Brandi," this voice belonged to Emily's art teacher Mrs. Nicole. "What are they going to do?"

"I heard they might have to take her to down to UC Davis for testing."

"Her parents must be terrified. That's twice in one week she's passed out."

Emily wanted to listen more, but her bus was waiting. She made some stomping noises with her feet in warning, and ran in the room past the huddled teachers who looked up in surprise.

"Sorry, forgot my homework."

She ran to the back table where art projects were kept, grabbed hers and headed to the door.

She tossed over her shoulder as she ran for the bus, "See ya tomorrow."

On the bus, she walked down the aisle toward the back. The bus picked up students from all of the surrounding towns between Interstate 80 and Loyalton. Like Calpine, Sadley and Chilcute, her town, Sierraville, was just a wide spot in the road. Its elementary school closed three years ago for lack of students, so the bus carried kids from kindergarten to high school. The little kids sat in the front and the older ones toward the back.

Since her mother recently started homeschooling her brothers, they weren't on her bus. She missed seeing the grins of Parker and Tayler as she walked by the little ones who were loaded on first. Her mom had pulled the boys from school when Parker came home with a bloody nose after a classmate teased him about Dawna. This left her family with less income from her mom's job as a clerk at the Country Grocery store, but Emily understood the decision. It was as if her family had pulled into a protective shell after Dawna left, and only their closest friends were allowed inside.

She made her way to her assigned seat next to Teddy. He was a tall, string bean of a kid Emily had known since kindergarten. They were often paired since Emily's last name was Jensen and Teddy's was Johnson. They'd been lab partners in middle school, and sat near each other whenever a seating chart was alphabetized, as it was on the school bus. Most people thought Teddy was odd-looking with his tightly curled blonde hair, blue eyes, and distinctly African features. He was African American, but his pale skin and hair indicated he was probably an albino. But Emily never bothered to clarify. Teddy's strange looks were not the only thing that made people shy away from him. Being black would have been enough to make Teddy stand out in this largely white rural town, but being albino was a double whammy. On top of that he was unnaturally quiet. He was so quiet it was disconcerting. Emily never called it shyness. Teddy would talk to her whenever the need arose, and without the apparent discomfort that shy people felt. No, he wasn't shy, he was just quiet. It was as if he saved his words for something more important. For Emily, in her current state, that made Teddy a perfect seatmate. She needed time to think about what she'd heard in the art room.

She reviewed what she knew. There was only one Brandi in their high school — Brandi Burges. Brandi would have been at the football practice because she was a cheerleader, and cheerleaders practiced whenever the team did. She herself had seen Brandi 'nearly comatose' on Monday. That meant this was the second time she'd had a...a what? Was it a seizure? Was it even a physical episode of some kind? Emily was stumped. When she'd come across her in the bathroom she felt that Brandi was scared, not hurt. At least not hurt *physically*. What could possibly be wrong with her? The whole school was talking about it, and when it came out Emily had been the one to find her in the bathroom, she'd been deluged with questions. She was able to shrug off most of them with a surly look or short retort. But, she couldn't stop thinking about it. *Why do I bother with her? Brandi would certainly never think twice about me.*

She looked over at Teddy who always sat next to the window. *Should I ask him what he thinks about Brandi?* He had his earbuds in and was listening to music, his blue eyes covered in sunglasses. *Nah, I don't want to bother him,* she decided. *Besides, that would be like gossip, and I've about had it with the gossip in this town! But what is happening to Brandi Burges?*

CHAPTER THREE
EMILY

ON FRIDAY, AFTER SCHOOL, Loyalton High was abuzz with excitement about the football game. It seemed all but one of the 130 students could speak of nothing else. Posters and slogans lined the orange and white hallways. It was a home game against the Big Valley Cardinals, and Grizzly fans were awash in a sea of blue and white. Even the weather had warmed in anticipation of the big game.

Emily didn't feel like going to the game that night. She was definitely in a funk. She missed Dawna, remembering how they attended games together and sometimes her whole family had come. She didn't have the energy to go and sit in the cold while people whispered about her. No, she'd just take the bus home and curl up in her warm bed. She smiled thinking of a good book and a bowl of mint chip ice cream.

She walked to the long row of blue lockers just inside the school entrance. As she opened her locker door, something fluttered to the ground. Picking it up, she unfolded the small, square, pink-colored note that someone had evidently pushed through the air vents. It read: "Meet me at the afterparty. I need to talk." It was signed, "Brandi."

Emily stood motionless staring at the paper in her hand. Had Brandi Burgess put this note in her locker? Could this be some kind of cruel joke? The more she thought about it, a joke didn't make sense. Why would Brandi harass Emily who had helped her up off the bathroom floor? No, it had to be a real note from her. Brandi wanted to talk to *her* after the game. *Why does she want to talk to me? Is she going to warn me to keep my mouth shut, or try to bribe me not to tell or...something?*

Now she knew she would have to go to the game to get to the afterparty, but how to get there? Her parents didn't have the gas money to drive her to games, and she didn't want to stay at school all afternoon. Her surly attitude had driven away any friends she'd once had, and that hadn't been many as she mostly hung out with Dawna and her friends.

She noticed Teddy at his locker down the line from hers. Did he go to football games? She tried to remember back to the few games she'd attended this year, but couldn't place him at one. He did live near her and it couldn't hurt to ask. Hesitantly she approached him.

"Hey, Teddy, are you going to the game tonight?"

Teddy looked startled that someone was speaking to him. He glanced down at Emily, and took his ever-present earbuds out of his ears.

"What?"

"Are you going to the game tonight?"

"Don't know," he said shrugging his shoulders.

She looked at him seriously for a moment not sure what to say next. She decided to be honest.

"I was looking for a ride."

"Oh, okay. I guess I'll go then."

"Can we stay for the afterparty for a while?"

"I guess so." He shrugged again.

She considered him. What did she really know about Teddy? He had always just been there, a part of her life, but not. Now she wondered if she'd missed something. Was Teddy slow? *No, not slow, I've seen him in classes. He's bright. He's just odd.*

She asked, "Well, when do you want to pick me up?"

"Six-thirty I guess."

"Okay, great. Thanks!"

They turned toward the bus at the same time, and Emily realized they now had a thirty-minute bus ride home together. *Awkward!*

IT WAS EVEN MORE AWKWARD LATER when Teddy's parents pulled up to her house to take them to the game. Neither she nor Teddy were old enough to drive, so she'd expected his Mom to come, but his mom and dad decided to watch the game too. She'd never met Teddy's dad before. He traveled the thirty odd miles to Truckee for work like many men in Sierraville, so he wasn't around much. Emily was slightly surprised because both of Teddy's parents were African American. On some level she must have known Teddy would have black parents but she thought his dad would also be albino. But here they were, both black, and Teddy sat next to her in the back seat with his blonde curls and white skin. She wondered how common albinos were and if Teddy had to be careful in the sun. What was it like for him at family reunions where he no doubt stood out as a white blip in a sea of black faces? Was his difference a part of what made him so quiet?

She realized just how little she had thought about Teddy before and felt bad for it. She frowned — *Is this who I am? So lost in my own family's drama I've become selfish and self-centered, never noticing or even wondering about other people?*

Teddy's mom, Doris, was warm and friendly. She had been a parent helper when Teddy and Emily were in third grade, and Emily remembered she made great chocolate chip cookies. Doris kept up a conversation with Emily that bypassed Teddy and his father. Emily thought it must be lonely living in a house with two quiet men. Her house was always full of noise with her little brothers around.

It was twilight, her favorite time of evening. Darkness came early in the shadow of the mountains. She starred out the window the thirteen miles into town. Miles and miles of pastures occasionally dotted with cows and old barns. The pine trees in the distance seemed dark and brooding in the failing light, but the pastures took on the magical greens and golds of the fading sun.

At the game, Doris put blankets down on the cold metal bleachers and handed out more to snuggle under. Teddy's parents sat together. Teddy sitting over next to his dad while she and Doris shared the same blanket as the evening chill set in. Emily found herself getting caught up in Doris' enthusiasm for the game, and for the first time in a long time she was actually enjoying herself. Friends came by to say hi to them. She wondered if being there with Teddy's family would start the gossip mill going. *Probably not*, she decided, *everyone here takes rides however they can get them. Besides, what's one more thing to be gossiped about?*

Emily kept her eyes trained on Brandi during most of the game. She was afraid Brandi would collapse mid-cheer and found herself feeling very protective. Besides, she wasn't hard to watch with her brown hair shining under the lights, bright white smile and large brown eyes. Emily couldn't stop herself from contrasting her looks to Brandi's. She paled in comparison. Her hair was brown, too, and similarly shoulder length, but seemed to hang in limp formation. She was shorter and thin, but in a gangly way, not the graceful way Brandi was. And she was definitely missing curves. *Would they come later?* she wondered.

Brandi's parents were sitting about three rows in front of Emily, to her right. Mr. Burges owned a popular restaurant up in Truckee, making their family one of the wealthier in the area. Emily noticed that Brandi's petite mother, who was Chinese, was also watching, and with worried eyes. Mrs. Burges's small size was deceptive; she had the reputation of being a strong woman, working tirelessly at the restaurant and volunteering at the school. Emily felt some kinship with Mrs. Bruges as they worried over Brandi together.

The afterparty was always held at the school. There really wasn't anywhere else in town big enough for all the students and their families. The party was especially loud because the Grizzly's won the game fourteen - zip. Families crowed the entrance of the school and overflowed into the gymnasium. The game smells of grass stains, hot dogs and tobacco followed the crowds into the warm school.

Emily's stomach began to knot after the game. What if Brandi was mad at her for being there when she was sick? What if she yelled at her? How was she going to approach Emily for their conversation? She didn't have to wait long. Soon after she and Teddy's family entered the building and headed for the refreshment table, Brandi moved away from her group of friends and over to Emily.

"Bathroom," was all she said.

Emily walked to the girl's bathroom, the scene of their first encounter. Glad to find the room empty, she braced herself for whatever would come next. Brandi followed her in and, after determining it to be empty, began speaking fast.

"I'm having trouble. I don't know what's happening to me, and my parents think I'm sick or crazy. They're not letting me out of their sight. Do you…do you know what's happening to me?"

Emily was not expecting this. How could she know what was happening to Brandi? She'd just been at the wrong place at the right time.

"Why would I know?" she asked, immediately regretting her tone.

"It's just that you seemed to understand, in some way — what I was going through. You being there that day — it helped."

Emily was shocked. Brandi was not going to yell at her after all, in fact, she was asking for help.

"I'm sorry, I really don't know. I wish I could help."

She saw the pleading look in Brandi's eyes. She wished she could offer more, but she had nothing else to give.

Brandi's eyes sparkled with tears of disappointment and frustration. She stood up tall, took a deep breath, and, nodding, turned to leave.

"Wait," said Emily, desperate to say something.

"What?"

"Well, if it helps, I don't think you're crazy. When I came in that day you seemed… well, terrified." Emily held her breath. Had she said too much?

Brandi looked at her curiously then she spoke in a whisper, "I was."

"If you ever need to talk about it or, if there's anything I can do to help, let me know."

Brandi nodded once, said a quick "Thanks", and then she turned and left the bathroom.

Emily leaned against the red and blue bathroom walls, starring at the grizzly paw prints on the stalls. What could she possibly do to help Brandi Burges?

CHAPTER FOUR
BRANDI

BRANDI WAS DEEP IN THOUGHT as she left the Blue Moon Bakery with two boxed pies for her father's birthday. The breeze carried the scent of pecan and cherry filling into her nose, and her stomach growled, momentarily distracting her from her ponderings. She was excited about the surprise she'd arranged for her father's birthday. He loved Vicky's pies!

She returned to her ruminations while walking up the sidewalk toward her car. Popularity! That's what she'd been thinking about. Why were some people popular and others not? She felt the burden of popularity as a physical weight pressing down on her shoulders. Sighing she grumbled in internal argument — *It's not my fault I was born pretty, smart or likeable, I just came out that way!* She was sick of trying to meet everyone's expectations; her mom wanted her to be a straight A student; her dad wanted an athlete. Her "friends" hounded her for fashion and makeup advice. She started trends without even trying — it was maddening! She didn't even really care about fashion or makeup.

If I can just survive this place until college! Here she was a big fish in a small pond. At college she could just blend in, fly under the radar. Here, her life was under a microscope, and the crowd could be fickle, just waiting for you to fall. She'd heard the whisperings: *Is Brandi doing drugs? Is she fainting because she's pregnant?* The piranhas were starting to swarm.

I wish I could just leave town like Dawna did. Just go somewhere and be anonymous. Thinking about Dawna reminded her of Dawna's little sister, Emily, who found her in the bathroom. She thought Emily was interesting. *Probably because she doesn't simper around me and cling to every word I say!* In fact, Emily did not use the bathroom incident to try to talk to her at all. *Probably has more interesting things to think about than me.*

She clicked the unlock sensor on her keys and opened the passenger-side door and carefully placed the pies on the seat. Worried what a sudden stop would do she moved them down to the floor mats.

Puffy white clouds skimmed the mountaintops and threw patterns of sunlight across her car. *What a beautiful day,* she thought circling to the driver's side and climbing in. Suddenly the sky went dark, or was it her eyes? She felt small and terrified. She was cold and began to shiver uncontrollably. *Oh no, it's happening again,* was her last coherent thought.

Now she was lying on an earth packed dirt floor shivering. Fear and panic were seizing her body, making it impossible to think. It was pitch black and she couldn't see anything; if only she could see. Her left arm hurt and was bent at an odd angle. *Breathe,* she told herself. *You need to figure out what's going on!* She was covered in something scratchy and wiggled around to try to get the scratchy thing off her body. She felt overwhelmed by a sudden fierce need to be out from under the scratchy – what – blanket? She thrashed and kicked. *Calm down,* she told herself. *Pay attention!*

She tried to get a sense of where she was. She breathed in through her nose, damp and stale...potatoes? Suddenly she heard a tapping sound.

CHAPTER FIVE
EMILY

"CHEEEP, CHEEEP, CHEEEP," rang Emily's house phone from her bedside table. Emily was leaning against her headboard Sunday night, lost in a novel, when the phone broke her concentration. Her parents let her answer the phone when it rang at night because no one called them after eight. She would have preferred a cell phone but they didn't have much cell coverage in Sierraville, and her parents, like most of the 380 residents, couldn't afford it anyway. She picked up the phone, surprised to see an unfamiliar number on the caller I.D.

"Hello."

"Emily?" the voice said.

It was a familiar voice but it took Emily a moment to place it. "Brandi?"

"Hi. I'm sorry to bother you."

"Uh, no bother."

"It's just…it happened again. I don't know who else to talk to." Her voice sounded weak and worried.

"Do you need me to come over?" The words were barely out of Emily's mouth before she regretted them. She had no way to get to Brandi's house, and the idea that Brandi would want her at her house, like a friend, was ludicrous.

"No, it's late. I just wondered if you could keep a secret."

Emily thought about this. It seemed that keeping secrets was what she was best at lately. Dawna had sworn her to secrecy about the details of her rescue and reminded her of that promise just today. Even her parents didn't know about it. During their much-anticipated weekly phone call, Dawna spoke one-on-one with each member of her family. When it was Emily's turn, Dawna told her astounding news. Last Monday, the first day at her new school, she had run into one of her rescuers! They'd been hanging out ever since. Her name is Sam and she was the girl who brought Dawna up to the house the night of her return. Emily actually met Sam that night, although Dawna said she now looked completely different, having cut her hair short and dyed it red. Emily could tell Dawna was glad to have found a friend.

Besides keeping her escape secret, Dawna's lawyer said they also had to keep all the details of the kidnapping secret, until after the trial, so as not to compromise the case. It felt to Emily that her head was swimming with secrets, and one more might just drown her.

But she said "Of course, it's what I'm best at," and heard Brandi sigh in relief.

"Okay. Well you can't tell anyone. I just don't know who else to talk to. This town is so small!"

"Tell me about it," agreed Emily.

"Yeah, I guess you understand more than anyone. I'm sorry Emily. I'm sorry Dawna had to leave. We used to be in ballet together when we were little. I'm sorry to burden you with my problems when you've got plenty of your own."

Emily was afraid Brandi might change her mind about talking to her so she cut in, "Really, it's no problem. Tell me about what happened, how did it start?"

This seemed to be all the encouragement Brandi needed. "Well, that's the hardest part. It's like there's no warning. Today I was out running errands in my car, and I suddenly got so afraid. I guess that's how it starts. This feeling of terror comes over me, and I know that's just the beginning. So, luckily, I had gotten back in the car when it happened and wasn't driving. But then, it's not like I blackout, exactly. I'm aware of what's happening the whole time. It's like I'm in two places at once. I know I'm in the car, but I feel like I'm locked in a small space somewhere else, too. I feel cold and wet and hungry and…well, terrified."

The phone went silent as Emily listened, waiting for Brandi to say more.

"My mom thinks I'm having panic attacks, and is going to take me out of school tomorrow to see a Doctor in Rancho Cordova. I Googled panic attacks, and I don't think that's what's happening to me. The thing is, I don't have any idea what *is* happening to me."

The phone was quiet again, and Emily had the feeling Brandi wanted her to say something, but she didn't know what to say. "Uh, what happened next, in the car I mean?"

"Well, I was curled up on the front seat in a ball. You know, like you found me in the bathroom. Vicky, who runs the bakery, came by and tapped on my window. That was embarrassing. It seems like that pulls me out of it, ya know. Like when you talked to me in the bathroom. I heard the tapping on the window, and was able to sit up. I rolled down the window, and she asked if I was all right. I'd just been in there picking up two of her amazing pies for my dad's birthday. So I lied and said I'd just dropped my keys!"

"Did she believe you?"

"I guess. I hate that this whole town knows there's something wrong with me. She asked if I was sure, so I said yes, and she went on her way, but she looked worried. It took me five minutes before I felt like I could drive. I felt really shaky afterwards."

"Are you okay now?"

"Yeah, I'm fine now. I feel perfectly normal. I just wanted to talk to someone about it. My parents are already totally freaked out and, you know, and I can't really tell my friends."

Emily knew exactly what Brandi was saying. It didn't bother her that she just implied they weren't friends. They *weren't* friends after all. She was already the victim of the gossip mill in this little valley. She didn't wish that on anyone.

"No, I get it," she said.

"So, do you have any theories?"

Emily wondered again why Brandi would think she would have theories. *Does being the victim of a crime, or the sister of the victim, suddenly make you the expert on all out-of-the-ordinary things that happen?*

"Brandi, I'm sorry. I really honestly have no idea." Emily felt like she was somehow letting Brandi down with this statement. What could she possibly say to help her? She cast around in her memory for any ideas. Then she stumbled on one. When Dawna was returned from the kidnappers, the victim's advocate who visited suggested she write a journal about what happened to her. Dawna seemed to take to that idea and filled a whole journal about her story.

"Brandi, why don't you try writing everything down?"

"What do you mean?"

"Well, write down what it feels like when this happens, all the details you can remember. Then, maybe we can talk about it and find some, I don't know, some clue as to why this is happening." Emily held her breath, feeling sure she'd just said the lamest thing ever to the most popular girl in her high school.

"That's a good idea!" Brandi sounded hopeful for the first time since the phone call began. "I'll write everything down. It's somewhere to start, and it will help me when I see the doctor. I'll do that right now. Thanks Emily."

The phone went dead and Emily looked at the receiver shaking her head. *Weird*, she thought. Was Brandi Burges cracking up?

CHAPTER SIX

EMILY

EMILY WOKE UP IN A COLD SWEAT. She'd had the strangest dream. It seemed so real. She had only experienced one other dream that felt this real in her whole life. It was the one she had the night before Dawna came home, about Sam bringing her home, and *that* was exactly what happened.

This dream was different, but had the same "real" kind of feeling to it. She lay in her bed remembering. The dream started with a feeling, more than a picture. The feeling was pure terror. It was dark in her dream, as if she'd entered a dark room, and her eyes hadn't adjusted. The room smelled of dirt, dampness and something else—was it potatoes? She'd heard a scuffling sound in the dark and jumped. Were there rats in this room, or something else, something worse? Jerking her head back and forth, she tried to see around the room. Slowly she could make out her surroundings. A little outside light seeped into the darkness illuminating a pile of rags on the floor. The bundle of rags was moving! She stepped back, her breath catching in her throat. It felt as if the bundle was pulling her in closer. She didn't want to go closer. Her heart thudded in her chest, but the pull was very strong. She took one step toward the dark bundle on the floor. Suddenly, a sharp scraping sound came up from behind her as a door was pulled open. She was trapped between the moving rags and whoever was coming down the stairs. Wood creaked as a foot stepped on the first stair. She held her breath.

In the dream, she knew that whatever was on the stairs was far worse than what was on the floor in front of her. She pushed her forearm over her mouth to keep herself from screaming.

Then, she was sitting upright in bed, her left arm aching where she'd sunk her teeth into it. Heart racing, she felt disoriented, unsure of where she was. Gradually she realized she was in her own room, the one she'd shared with Dawna. Her heart slowed a little as she began to calm down.

What was this dream about? Was Dawna okay? Or was her dream related to what Brandi told her about being terrified? Had she incorporated Brandi's fears into her own dreams? No, the last time she'd had a dream this real, it was about Dawna. What if Dawna was hurt? Finally, she could think of only one thing to do. She dialed Dawna's cell phone number.

"Hello," croaked a sleepy voice on the other end of the line.

"Dawna, it's me. Are you okay?"

"Em, its four o'clock in the morning. Why are you calling me to ask if I'm okay? I was fine until you woke me up!"

"I'm sorry, it's just that I had this dream, and it freaked me out."

Emily could hear Dawna sit up in her bed. She sounded more awake now and very concerned, "Okay, tell me about your dream."

ON THE SCHOOL BUS THE NEXT DAY Teddy sat studying Emily. He'd been studying her since kindergarten although she had no clue how much time and energy she occupied in his life. He loved her, but he would never tell her. Emily was the one person in his life, outside of his parents, who never looked at him strangely. She looked at him like she looked at everybody, as something outside of her concern. He imagined it was sad that her indifference was the closest he'd come to positive interest from a girl. He felt safe and comfortable around her indifference. With everyone else he felt anxious, even fearful, but not with Emily. Sometimes she even talked to him; he lived for those days.

Today, Emily was struggling to keep her eyes open. She must have felt him looking at her because she sat up straighter, with a quizzical look on her face. He pulled the earbuds out of his ears.

"You okay?" he asked.

"Rough night."

He wasn't buying it. There was something she wasn't telling him. He continued to stare at her, hoping she'd share more, but she didn't. He decided there was only one thing he could do. He knew he shouldn't but Emily was important to him. She was one of the few people in his world that treated him like a normal person. He reached out his left hand, and let it sit on top of her right one. Suddenly he was flooded by intense sensory impressions: fear, friendship, darkness, and a musty smell. What was it, potatoes? He quickly pulled his hand away, lost in the rush of information her skin had downloaded into his body. At first, he didn't hear her voice.

"Teddy?"

His eyes refocused on her. Her eyebrows were almost touching each other and her eyes were glaring at him with angry intensity. What had she thought, that he was trying to hold her hand? He realized he'd better clear things up right away.

"You're very worried about something. Someone you know is very, very scared."

"What?" she asked in disbelief. "How do you know that?"

"I just know. Is it Dawna? Is she okay?"

"She's okay." Emily looked touched by his concern. "I talked to her last night."

"Then who is it?" He looked directly at her with his ice blue eyes.

Emily didn't answer. He knew she'd tell him when and if she wanted him to know. He had already forced his way into her feelings and, as his mother would say, that was a "no-no."

CHAPTER SEVEN

SAMMY

TWO WEEKS EARLIER

SAMMY WAS LOST IN THOUGHT as she walked down the hill to McQueen High School in Reno. She felt she'd spent most of the fall lost in thought, but there was so much to think about. Right now she was thinking about her friends. At the end of their summer school class she, Ty, Tiff, and Lando agreed to defy the odds and keep the "Blue group" together, despite Mr. Monahan's warnings that some groups were only meant to be together for a short time. They knew their group was different. Wasn't it The Blues working together to rescue Dawna from the kidnappers? Wasn't it their group that helped break up the ring of truck-stop sexual slavery? They grew so close they could trust each other with everything. They had even seen supernatural things happen. You would think it would be enough to keep a group of friends from growing apart, but apparently it wasn't.

They did still have their monthly lunch date; it was Lando's idea. They met the first Sunday of every month for lunch no matter what. Of course, Lando originally suggested a weekly meeting, but when they compared schedules, monthly was all they could agree on. Now even that sacred date was beginning to slip through their fingers. Tiff missed the September meeting when her tennis team was out of town for finals. Ty missed the October meeting for a National Science Fair competition. Sam wondered if Tiff and Ty were avoiding each other. Their budding romance was cut short by Tiff's families' drastic over-reaction when Ty invited her to attend the Hug High homecoming dance. Tiff was very excited to go but her parents said absolutely not. They said she was "too young to date," but Tiff confessed to Sammy, during a teary phone call, that perhaps their reaction had more to do with Ty's ethnicity than *her* age. It was bad enough that Tiff wanted to date a non-Korean, but a black man? Tiff said she could read the truth in their eyes and she was heartbroken.

Tiff seemed to deal with this hurt by pouring herself even more into sports. Ty was dealing with it, according to Lando, by becoming suddenly interested in his lab-partner, Sheila. Now Tiff and Ty were avoiding each other. Sammy and Tiff still talked on the phone and Lando wrote Sammy on Facebook all the time, but she couldn't help thinking their group was slowly dissolving.

Lando was another story. Last summer Tiff suggested Lando would make a good lawyer, and now it was all he could think about. He'd stopped playing video games and taken to reading John Grisham novels. He went so far as to join the debate team, and he loved it.

Well, that will probably keep him from making this weekend's lunch date. Sammy felt bitterness dampen her mood and she kicked at a rock on the sidewalk in front of her.

Pausing next to the bus stop halfway to campus, she pictured her summer school teacher, Mr. Monahan flying down the hill on his longboard and ending up head first in the bushes. She was not actually there to see this happen, but Mr. Monahan's recounting of the story was as vivid in her mind as if she *had* seen it. The imagined scene made her smile, lifting her sour mood.

She loved Mr. Monahan's summer school class and was sorry her grades weren't good enough to be in his honors English this year. But, she realized happily, her grades had improved pretty drastically since last year. She had also been inspired by Tiff's pronouncement she would make a great art teacher. Something in that short statement took root in Sammy's heart and started to grow. For the first time she felt her life might have meaning.

She glanced down at her boots, long and black, but that was the only black she was wearing today. Since this summer, she'd decided she would use this year to experiment with who she wanted to be instead of allowing herself to be defined by what had been done to her in the past. So far, she found she really liked colors. This was no surprise to anyone else of course, artists liked colors, and it made sense. She had spent the fall combing thrift shops, and now owned quite an eclectic, and colorful, wardrobe. Today, in honor of the crisp fall air, she wore tall black boots. Her legs were warm in red leggings topped by a forest green, long sleeve, button-down men's shirt that covered her small frame like a dress. She layered that with a multi-colored tapestry vest. On her head was a brown crushed velvet tam. The tam and the vest were two of her favorite finds at the thrift store. Yes, today she was even happy with her hair. She'd been experimenting with different colors and somehow felt red suited her pale skin.

I shouldn't let them bother me! She chastised herself thinking again of her friends. The problem was she didn't really have any other friends, and these three friends were extremely important to her. The friendship was probably more important to her than it was to any of the other group members. Tiff had her sports; Lando his debate group; Ty had Sheila. But who did she have?

Sammy was still pondering these thoughts as she arrived at her homeroom class. Pulling out her art book, she began shading in her latest assignment. This year, in addition to being her art teacher's aide, she was also taking advanced art, and she loved it. Students settled in around her. They laughed and talked easily about their weekends. She had the distinct feeling, that came on her occasionally, that she was years older than her peers. She wanted friends, but she didn't know how to relate to people her age. Their concerns seemed foreign to her: dances, dates, television shows? These things held no interest for Sammy who preferred reading, drawing and writing poetry. People didn't shy away from her as in past years, but they weren't exactly inviting her over, either.

A hush fell over the class and Sammy glanced up to see a new girl enter the room escorted by one of the school counselors. She was pretty with short blonde hair. Sammy immediately wrote her off as a popular type and went back to drawing. Her concentration was broken again when her desk was hit by the new student's backpack as she plopped into the desk to Sammy's left. The jarring caused her shading pencil to make a black line outside of her drawing. Irritated she looked up at new girl who had muttered a hasty apology. Their eyes met and realization hit Sammy like a pail of ice water. Dawna was staring back at her.

Sammy hadn't seen Dawna since that night last summer when they'd rescued her from the kidnappers and taken her home. She couldn't believe she was seeing her now. Recognition had not registered in Dawna's eyes as it had in Sammy's. She realized Dawna had only seen her in a drug-induced haze and with long black hair. Flipping a page in her art book she hastily wrote, "It's me, Sammy, from last summer."

Slowly Dawna's eyes grew large and her mouth fell open. Pulling out a notebook, she scribbled a line, holding it up for Sammy to see.

"I thought I dreamed you."

Sammy wrote back, "What are you doing here?"

Dawna whispered, "Let's talk after class."

Sammy couldn't focus on her drawing any more, and started packing up her things before the morning bell signaled the end of homeroom. Soon, she and Dawna were huddled together outside the front door as hoards of students hurried past them.

"I'm so glad to see a friendly face," said Dawna. "This place is huge!"

"Where's your next class?

Dawna pulled out her class schedule and consulted it.

"I have English with Mr. Monahan in room 103."

"Are you kidding me? He's my favorite teacher! Well, one of them anyway. I'll walk you. It's on the way to my math class."

As they walked, Dawna talked as fast as she could.

"I can't believe you're here. I can't even believe you are real. I honestly thought maybe I'd dreamed you and the others. Are they here too?"

"No, they all go to other high schools."

"Oh, too bad, I would love a chance to thank them. Anyway, it's really good to see you."

They came to a stop outside Mr. Monahan's classroom.

"Dawna, can we meet for lunch?" Sammy asked.

"That would be great. I feel so lost here. Where should I meet you?"

"Head to the cafeteria, and look for me by the table under the Lancer mural."

"What's a Lancer?"

"It's a knight. It's our school mascot." Sammy rolled her eyes at the lameness of it.

They were interrupted when Mr. Monahan poked his head out of the classroom looking for lingering students.

"Oh. Hey Sam, how are you?"

"I'm great Mr. Monahan." She said smiling, honestly glad to see him again. Then she remembered the girl standing next to her. "This is Dawna. She's new, and she's in your class."

"Nice to meet you, Dawna," he held out his hand and Dawna shook it. "Go on in and find a seat." Dawna went into the classroom with a nod back at Sammy.

Sammy returned the nod and started to leave.

Mr. Monahan's voice stopped her. "Hey Sam, I was hoping to see you sometime. I was wondering if you'd be willing to draw up some sketches for our spring musical."

"Me?"

"Yep, we're doing *The Man of La Mancha*. Ever heard of it?"

"No."

"Well, I was remembering that dragon and knight you drew on your notebook last summer, and I thought you might be interested in helping us with some of our set pieces."

"Well, sure. I guess." Sammy could not remember ever being asked to do anything for a teacher before. Except her art teacher.

"Great! Wait right here and I'll grab you a script." He popped back into his classroom as the bell rang.

Sammy started to fidget nervously. She couldn't afford to be late for math. She already knew Mrs. Hoy didn't like her.

Mr. Monahan was back in a flash. He was so tall he practically had to duck to get through the door.

"Here it is Sam. We're having a read through next Monday after school, and we start rehearsals then if you'd like to join us. I'd love to hear your ideas for some of the set pieces."

"Uh, that'd be cool I guess..." Sammy had never been involved in an extra-curricular school activity. What was happening to her? A lunch date and an extra-curricular all in one day?

"And here Sam," he handed her a small slip of paper. "It's a pass so you won't get in trouble for being late."

"Thanks." Sammy smiled in relief and headed to class.

AT THE LUNCH TABLE DAWNA had been talking non-stop. Sammy felt happier than she had in a long time, since summer, she realized. *This must be what it feels like to have friends at school.* Sammy never lived anywhere long enough to have school friends.

"So I just couldn't take it anymore," Dawna continued. "When you go to school with the same 130 kids your whole life, and they decide you're shady...well."

"It sucks," finished Sammy.

"Yeah, it sucks. Anyway, that's how I got here. Tell me about you and your friends. I was so out-of-it that night, I don't remember much. You know they had me drugged right?"

"We figured it out."

"Well, I remember hitting the ground after that guy threw me out of his truck for not having sex with him. That hurt! And, I remember the car chase vaguely. I remember you guys cleaning me up and buying me food. That was really nice. I thought you were angels. I mostly remember you going with me into the house. You didn't have to do that."

"I just wanted to be sure you were okay."

"Thanks, I was. But like I told you, what's happened since has been almost as hard."

"Yeah, I can relate to that." Sammy picked at her sandwich, her smile fading.

"You said something like that had happened to you, didn't you?"

"*Something* like that."

Dawna sat quietly waiting for Sammy to continue. Sammy felt bad; she knew she should let Dawna off the hook and just tell her what happened. But this friendship was so new and she didn't want to ruin it, before it even started. What if Dawna heard her story and rejected her?

Dawna kindly changed the subject. "So, what about your friends who were with you that night...do you still see them?"

Sammy felt even sadder. "Not as much as I'd like. We see each other about once a month. Hey! We're having lunch this Sunday. You should come. They'd love to see you."

"Seriously? That would be great." Dawna beamed at Sammy, and she felt her heart begin to glow.

CHAPTER EIGHT
EMILY

FRIDAY WAS A GOOD DAY for Emily. In fact, it was a great week. She hadn't any more bad dreams, and as far as she knew, Brandi was episode free. No one talked to her about the trial, and Teddy was keeping his hands to himself. She shivered remembering how he seemed able to read her feelings when he touched her. Neither of them had talked about it since. She didn't know what to say so she avoided him at school and stuck her nose in a book on the bus.

The best news of the week was that Dawna would be coming home this weekend. She was bringing Sam, who'd helped rescue her, but Emily was told to pretend she was meeting Sam for the first time. Dawna didn't want her folks to figure out who she was. She and her friends wanted to keep their part in Dawna's rescue a secret. Emily wasn't sure why; it had something to do with how they got the information to rescue Dawna in the first place. Her sister implied it came to them *supernaturally* and the cops would never buy that explanation, so it was better not to bring it up.

Emily wondered what "supernaturally" meant. She was beginning to think the world was not as black and white as she'd originally supposed. Strange things were happening all over the place, Brandi was having weird episodes, she had strange dreams and Teddy, mister unremarkable, suddenly seemed to have ESP or something! What was going on here? Now she was supposed to pretend not to recognize Sam, because of something "supernatural." Emily shook her head, trying to clear it from all the tangles she felt in her mind.

Dawna said her folks would never recognize Sam, who they were to call "Sammy," as she looked completely different. That, and the fact their only glimpse of her was in the middle of the night when she brought Dawna home, should help. They'd been groggy and overwhelmed with emotion at seeing Dawna again. It would be enough to keep them from identifying Sammy with the rescue. She'd been in their home about three minutes total. And, as Emily recalled, she'd had long, jet black hair hanging over her eyes, no makeup and was wearing pajama pants and a huge sweatshirt. She looked about twelve. Nope, this deception would be a piece of cake. From Dawna's description, there was no way her folks would connect Sam to the Sammy that was coming.

Just before the last bell of the day rang, an office aide slipped into class and handed the teacher a note. Mrs. Nicole glanced at it quickly then dropped it on Emily's desk.

It said, "Come to the office to meet with Mrs. McWilliams after school." Emily didn't know who Mrs. McWilliams was, and that was saying a lot for someone living in such a small town. She tried to think if she'd done something to get in trouble, but couldn't come up with anything. *Is Dawna hurt? What about the boys, Mom and Dad?* Thankfully, the bell rang, and Emily quickly headed for the office.

She was met by a very short, round lady with eggplant-colored hair.

"Hello Emily," she said, leading her back toward the principal's office. "I'm Mrs. McWilliams, the district counselor. Have a seat."

Emily sat down in the only chair available that wasn't behind the principal's desk.

"Let me begin by apologizing for not having come to talk to you sooner. With an entire district, and only one counselor, things can be a bit hectic." She smiled at Emily, unaware that purple lipstick was marking her front teeth. "Of course I'm here to check on how your family's..." here she stopped to search for an appropriate word, "tragedy, is affecting you."

Emily's fragile happiness washed away with this one awkward sentence. She didn't know how to respond, or what was expected of her. She sat silently avoiding the lipsticked smile until realizing Mrs. McWilliams was waiting her out.

"I'm going to miss my bus."

"Oh, it's no problem. I contacted your mother and she will come into town at five to pick you up. She said you could wait over at the bakery, and she'd pay for whatever you ate when she got there."

Emily thought this over. Her mother couldn't afford gas into town let alone "whatever she ate at the bakery." She must be worried about Emily to agree to this interview. Or, more likely, the counselor called about talking to Emily, and her mother felt she would be considered uncaring if she said no. Her mother was too busy with her own grief from Dawna's moving and caring for the boys to notice

Emily these days. Her thoughts were interrupted when Mrs. McWilliams spoke again.

"The trial will be starting soon and I'm sure its bringing up lots of feelings for you. Would you like to talk about that?"

Emily felt her temper, which had dropped down to simmer lately, flare up again.

"No, I wouldn't, actually. I'm fine, and I'd be much happier if people stopped trying to get me to talk about it at all!" She jumped up out of the chair, grabbed her backpack and stomped out the door before Mrs. McWilliams could even protest. Rounding the office door, she bumped into Brandi Burges who was holding a note very similar to the one Emily received.

"Sorry," she said automatically. She and Brandi never talked to each other at school and acted like they didn't know each. Now, Brandi broke that unspoken rule.

"Do you know what this is about, Em?"

Emily was taken aback. Only Dawna called her Em. It was her special name for Emily. It shook her so much, she almost forgot to answer.

"District counselor, I guess we are both sick enough to get the honor of a visit!"

Brandi's face drooped and her eyes rolled. "Well, better get this over with." Taking a deep breath, she turned and walked into the office.

Emily marched out the front door of the school and to her surprise, found Teddy leaning on the Loyalton High sign.

"What are you doing here?" she barked. Then, realizing Teddy had done nothing to deserve her wrath quickly added, "Did you miss the bus?"

Teddy seemed unaffected by her shortness.

"No, I jumped off when I saw you weren't on it. I was afraid you'd try to hitch home alone. That's probably not such a good idea these days."

Emily's head was full of angry retorts. *What, you don't think I can take care of myself? Who named you my personal bodyguard?* But, she realized, she was touched by this gesture. Of all the people in her world, Teddy seemed the only one paying attention to her. He noticed her lack of sleep, and commented on her concern for a friend, *though how he knew that I'll never know,* and he was waiting for her now. She didn't feel angry anymore.

"Thank you Teddy. I'm supposed to wait for my mom at the Bakery till five, but if you're up for it, we could hitch together."

"Sure, or I could call my mom to come get us."

A brisk fall wind had come up and Teddy looked underdressed for it. But Emily didn't want to wait for his mom to come all the way into town to get them.

"Nah, I don't want to bother her."

Just then the door behind them banged open. Brandi came out looking livid.

Guess that went about as well as my interview, thought Emily.

Brandi glanced at Emily and Teddy then stormed past them to the parking lot in front of the school. She'd gotten all the way to her blue 4-wheel drive when she turned back to them.

"You two want a ride?"

"Sure," said Emily, grabbing Teddy's arm and dragging him toward the car. She felt so cool to be offered a ride by a popular senior. Did this mean Brandi was willing to make the fact they talked known to the outside world? When they were within a few feet of the car Brandi asked, "You're Teddy, right?"

"Teddy Johnson." Teddy held out his hand and Brandi shook it. Emily opened the front passenger door and jumped in, but Teddy was standing outside, looking up at the sky, a faraway look in his eye. Emily opened the door again; she had seen this look on Teddy's face once before, that morning on the bus when he touched her hand. It freaked her out. "Teddy, get in the car."

Teddy shook his head, slowly opened the back door and got in.

As Brandi was buckling her seatbelt, Teddy said, "You're the friend Emily's been worried about."

Brandi's head jerked toward Emily, "What? Emily, I told you those things in secret!"

"No," Emily's voice held panic, "I never told Teddy anything. I haven't told anyone!" Emily saw Brandi's fragile trust disintegrate before her eyes.

"Right, I should have known better than to trust anyone in this town." She started the car engine.

Teddy reached up from the back seat, and touched Brandi's shoulder.

"Don't blame Emily she hasn't said anything to me. I could just tell."

Brandi turned off the engine and unbuckled her seatbelt so she could turn around toward Teddy. "What is that supposed to mean?"

"Yeah, what *is* that supposed to mean Teddy?" added Emily, following Brandi's example and turning around.

Teddy looked like a blue-eyed deer caught in headlights. He chewed his lower lip. The girl's eyes pierced him while he sat trying to decide how much to say.

He began tentatively, "I sometimes sense…what others are feeling, when I touch them."

Emily and Brandi continued to stare at him, waiting for an explanation. He tugged on a stray blonde curl as he spoke.

"The other day, on the bus, Emily looked stressed. I touched her hand, and knew she was worried about a friend who was scared. Then, when you and I shook hands, I knew her friend was you." He gave his head a little nod, as if this was the most normal explanation in the world.

The girls continued to stare at him. Brandi turned to Emily,

"That make any sense to you?"

"The part about the bus is true. I just thought it was weird. I didn't know he could do it with everyone."

"I can't," Teddy corrected, "just…if there is a lot of emotion."

"Okay," said Brandi. "We'll test this, and see if you're both lying." She climbed up with her knees on the seat so her body faced Teddy. Brandi's silky brown hair shown in the afternoon sunlight that reflected in through the windshield. She reached her hands up over the seat toward him, fixing him with her lovely brown eyes. "Take my hands and see what you can tell me about what I've been going through."

Teddy gulped, reaching his pale hands up to grasp hers.

Dang, thought Emily, her heart going out to Teddy. *There's not a boy in school that wouldn't gladly trade places with him right now, but he looks like he's in pain.*

Teddy held Brandi's hands, and closed his eyes for a long moment. Brandi looked over at Emily, and raised one eyebrow, suggesting she didn't believe any of this.

Finally, Teddy opened his eyes and looked up at the girls. Brandi pulled her hands away.

"Brandi," he began in a careful voice, "you're small, cold and damp. You're trapped in a small dark room. And, you're terrified."

Brandi glared at Emily, "I told you all that."

Teddy went on unhindered, "You are covered in dirty, scratchy rags."

Brandi's breath sucked in, she looked at Emily, eyes wide. "I didn't tell you that!"

Emily's eyes narrowed as she looked at Teddy, "You see a rag pile in a dark room?"

Teddy nodded.

Emily looked from one to the other, "I had a dream about that, the night after you called Brandi, before Teddy touched my hand on the bus."

"You dreamed about the rags?" asked Brandi.

"Yes, it was terrifying. But I didn't tell Teddy anything about the dream."

Brandi looked interested. "Teddy, take Emily's hands and tell me what you see."

Teddy held Emily's hands and closed his eyes. Emily noticed his hands were unusually warm. When he looked up again, he let go of Emily's hands. "Someone is coming down the stairs into the dark room, a bad person."

Emily and Brandi both gasped and nodded in stunned silence.

CHAPTER NINE
DAWNA

DAWNA FELT HER SOUL EXPAND as she drove the borrowed red Honda Element up the mountains. It was thirty miles from Reno to the Sierraville turnoff and home! She'd only been gone two weeks but it felt like forever. So much had happened in those two weeks. She glanced over at Sammy who was starring wide-eyed at the forested hills. She seemed to be soaking in the beauty of the Sierra Mountains, so Dawna let her sit and kept her thoughts to herself.

She felt incredibly lucky to have met Sammy her first day at McQueen High School. She remembered feeling as lost as a country mouse when she first came to Reno. Her Aunt Jackie and Uncle Roy welcomed her warmly; in fact it was their car she was driving now. She felt calmer these days, but remembered the terror of her first day of school. Loyalton was a school of less than 200 kids and McQueen had two thousand! Her heart was pounding as she walked into her homeroom. Then, she accidently bumped the desk of the girl next to her and the rest was history.

They'd been fast friends ever since, spending every afternoon at Sammy's apartment. They had a routine now. She'd sit on Sammy's bed, propped on pillows against the corner wall reading books for Mr. Monahan's advanced English class. Sammy lay on the bed next to her, usually drawing. Her little sister, Charity, was lying on the floor next to the bed coloring, or singing, or playing with her Barbies'. In this way they'd built their friendship and it gave Dawna an anchor in the sea of faces of McQueen.

Sammy turned her pixie face to Dawna now, "Do you know I've only been up here in the daytime once?"

"Really? My family comes down to Reno a lot, mostly to see my aunt and uncle."

Sammy smiled, "I came once in the daytime to look for you and once in the middle of the night to find you!"

Dawna was still blown away by this information. Sammy was one of four students who'd met in Mr. Monahan's summer school English class. They came from four different high schools but bonded when they started getting "unexplained" information on who Dawna was and why she needed rescuing. Sammy took Dawna with her to meet the other members of the Blue Group one Sunday after her first week in Reno. She'd questioned them extensively about how they came to rescue her, but they were as mystified about it as she was. In the end, they settled on the term "supernatural information."

"Well I'm sure glad you did," she stated firmly.

"Me too," agreed Sammy happily. "I still don't understand why you ran away in the first place. From the stories you tell me, you love your family, no one has abused you, and you had good friends."

Dawna understood her confusion. Sammy came from a long history of living with a mom who drank and a string of awful stepfathers. One of them was in jail for abusing her. To her, Dawna's life must seem perfect.

She tried to explain, "Maybe you'll understand when you see my town. I know it was stupid now, but at the time I felt completely trapped. I mean, can you imagine going to school with the same kids your whole life?" As soon as the words left her mouth, Dawna knew it was the wrong thing to say. Of course Sammy couldn't imagine being raised with the same kids; she'd spent her entire life moving.

"Sorry, can't," said Sammy without anger. "McQueen's the first school I've been at two years in a row."

"I'm sorry Sammy; it must seem lame after what you've been through. Even my kidnapping was mild compared to what happened to you. I got rescued in time. You had to live through the abuse. I feel guilty even going to court when the other girls went through so much more than I did."

The girls were quiet for a time, each lost in their own thoughts. Then Dawna asked, "Did you have to testify in court?"

"I did. It was terrifying. But, I was only twelve, you'll be fine."

"I'm afraid of the cross examination part. They are going to try to discredit me. My case is the weakest of the three."

"Well, I guess the most important thing is that those guys get put away."

"Yeah, but I'd really like them to be convicted on my charges too. You know, my family believes me, but it would be validation, you know, to have guilty counts on my charges. I mean, I wasn't there as long as the other girls, and I wasn't raped, but, I *was* kidnapped. It did hurt me and disrupt my whole life."

"You're right Dawna. It is important. All three of you deserve justice!"

"Yeah, and it wouldn't hurt to have my name cleared around town, if you know what I mean. I feel so stupid for what I did and for the pain it caused my family. I almost wish something worse *had* happened to me.

"Don't say that," said Sammy grabbing Dawna's arm. "It's impossible to compare abuse in terms of levels. All abuse is wrong and evil."

Dawna felt her eyes fill with tears; she blinked rapidly to clear them so she could see to drive. Sammy's comment touched a nerve in her. She needed the court to vindicate her too; she needed her pain to be validated.

"Thanks Sammy, I needed to hear that."

CHAPTER TEN
EMILY

THE INTRODUCTION TO EMILY'S FAMILY went smoothly. Sammy wore her brightest clothes and even more makeup than usual. Her short, red hair and new name must have sealed the deal because there was no hint of recognition from Emily's parents or brothers. Emily did a good job of acting like she was meeting her for the first time. She watched as Sammy interacted with her parents. *I don't think I would have recognized her if I didn't know she was coming. It's not just her new fashion and hair, she seems lighter somehow, much more confident. She's had quite a change in her life I'd say.*

The day had been full of food and family. At eight o'clock, the boys were heading to bed, and Emily's parents were settling in for the night. Dawna, Sammy and Emily got into the car, supposedly heading out to visit some of Dawna's high school friends. They really went to Teddy's house. Emily explained that she and her friends had some issues they needed Dawna and Sammy's help with. Even though she'd told Dawna a little, she knew it was a shock when those "friends" turned out to be Teddy Johnson and Brandi Burges. It was a very unlikely gathering in Teddy's basement that night.

Teddy's mom made some of her delicious chocolate chip cookies and seemed very excited Teddy was having friends over. Emily could tell she wanted to stay and visit with them, but she left after reassuring Dawna several times it was good to see her, and the town was pulling for her. Everyone was introduced to Sammy and settled down on the comfortable couches in the cozy basement room. It was big and square with a large flat screen TV, stacks of movies, and several gaming systems. Emily couldn't help but think Teddy would have more friends if they knew what a cool set up he had at home.

When they were settled, Emily jumped right in aware it was already late. "Sammy, I've told Teddy and Brandi the little I know about what happened last summer and how you guys found Dawna."

Dawna sat up quickly, starting to speak.

"Wait," Emily said. "I had to tell them and, trust me, they will tell no one."

Dawna relaxed a little.

"The thing is, Brandi's been having some really strange things happening to her, and we were wondering if maybe, you could help her Sammy."

"Me?" Sammy asked in disbelief.

"Well, no pressure. It's just that we don't know where else to turn, and it sounds like you and your friends have been through some… odd things."

Sammy looked doubtful, but Emily continued. "We don't have a lot of time, so we thought we'd summarize. Then, if you have any ideas that could help us, you could share them."

Sammy shrugged, "Okay."

Emily quickly summarized about Brandi's episodes, her dreams, and Teddy's ability to feel other's experiences through touch. Dawna and Sammy listened intently. Then all eyes turned on Sammy, expectantly.

"I can't believe this is happening to someone else. We thought it was just a fluke, a one-time thing. They're not going to believe this." She shook her head, lost in thought. "I really wish the Blue Group were here to hear this!"

"Let me just think a minute. I am familiar with the dream part. Ty had the dreams in our group. Emily, your dreams are as detailed as his were. You say you had another one last night and got even more information?"

"That's right. My dream last night started the same way the first one did, with terror. I walked toward the moving rags, and someone opened the door up the stairs behind me. I went to crouch down behind a rain barrel full of old potatoes, and I could see the moving rags more clearly. The size of the pile was small. No bigger than a dog, or a child. Then I woke up."

Sammy looked thoughtful, "Last summer, Ty's dreams were backed up by my drawings. Have any of you been drawing anything unusual lately?"

No one spoke. They all just shook their heads.

Dawna broke the silence, "Well, maybe it doesn't have to be drawing. Brandi's 'episodes' seem to back up Emily's dreams. Except maybe it's the opposite. Emily's dreams are backing up Brandi's episodes. And Teddy is confirming them through his ability to feel things."

The room was silent as everyone thought this through, then Brandi spoke.

"That would make me a lot happier than thinking I'm going crazy or have a brain tumor or something. When this was happening to you, did you figure out why or where it was coming from?"

Sammy's brow wrinkled, "Well, not exactly. We researched different things about dreams, and even interviewed people to get their opinions. In the end, we decided it was supernatural information."

Emily's eyebrows rose, "Supernatural information? You mean, like, from God? What kind of God would let my sister get kidnapped or put Brandi through this?"

Sammy shrugged her shoulders.

"Why would God be doing this to me?" Brandi asked, despair in her voice.

Sammy's mouth twitched sideways as she tried to formulate her thoughts. "It's not like God is the one doing this to people, it's just that there are bad people in the world and…bad stuff happens. I actually can't believe I am defending God. I blamed him for my own problems in the past, but the experience we had last summer has changed my thinking. He's the one that gives you the information to help. It's like a girl in our summer school class said, 'If God was going to give you powers, it would be to do things like he would do, like help someone.'"

Teddy spoke for the first time, "What do you mean *powers*?"

Sammy looked like her brain was starting to hurt. "Teddy, it was more like gifts. My friend Tiff found this verse in the Bible that said something about in the end of time God would pour out his gifts on all people, and they would have dreams and visions and stuff."

"Acts 2:17-18 quoted from the book of Joel," said Teddy.

"How did you know that?" asked Emily.

"Mom's a Sunday school teacher. She's always made me memorize verses. So Sammy, you think that's what's happening here? God is pouring his spirit out on us."

"I have no idea Teddy; I just know what we experienced. The things that happened to us were definitely *outsider* information and they led us to being able to rescue Dawna. That is the only thing I'm sure of."

Again the room fell silent. A realization began to dawn on them. Brandi was the first to voice it. "We're supposed to rescue someone trapped in a basement?"

"A child?" added Emily.

"I feel sick," said Teddy.

Brandi turned to Sammy, leaning forward. "How are we supposed to find the child? Should we call the police, what should we do?"

"That's the hard part," said Sammy. "If you tried to tell someone, they'd think you were crazy. We just had to wait until we were given more information. We had a "knower" in our group. Lando would get these feelings about when it was time to act. He just knew. But other information came from Ty's dreams and my drawings."

Emily cheered up, "Teddy knows things by touching people." She drooped again, "But what can we do with that? He can't just go around town touching everyone." The idea of Teddy walking around the small towns of Sierraville and Loyalton, touching people, was enough to bring the first smiles of the night.

Brandi looked at her watch, "Unfortunately, I'm on a short rope right now with my folks, and need to get home. Thanks, though, for coming Sammy and Dawna, too. I'm not glad I've been chosen, or whatever, but I am glad I'm not going crazy. At least we have something to work with, some idea of maybe what's happening." She turned to Teddy and Emily, "We're going to have to meet again soon. Let's think of a way to do that without raising suspicion."

Emily knew what that meant. They had to keep this from Brandi's friends.

CHAPTER ELEVEN
DAWNA

DAWNA'S CALL TO GO to Sacramento to testify against the kidnappers came Tuesday night. Two days after their return from Sierraville, they were headed over the mountain again. Sammy and Lando were traveling with Dawna. Sammy said Lando had gone "lawyer crazy" ever since a comment Tiffany made last summer, and when he heard they were going to the trial, he'd begged to come along.

Dawna's aunt, Jackie, drove them over the mountain. They had to leave at six o'clock in the morning to get to the courthouse by eight-thirty. The sun rose as they were hitting the 7200 foot summit of the mountain, and it was breathtaking. The deciduous trees, sprinkled in among the pines were mostly bare, but some still displayed colorful leaves. They added accent to the different green shades of conifers packed onto the mountainside.

The conversation was surprisingly fun. Dawna's aunt was a relaxed ex-hippy who had a playlist of mellow old rock music. Lando entertained Dawna and Sammy by keeping them all laughing the whole way. Dawna was grateful for Lando as he distracted her thoughts from the trial. *I like him!* She realized. But it was becoming obvious Sammy liked him more. *I wonder if she's even aware of it.*

Lando had arrived in a black suit, white shirt and black tie. He said it was important to "respect the court." Dawna and Sammy decided to wear skirts and blouses as Dawna's advocate said it was best to "dress semi-professionally."

The spiffy clothes made the whole thing feel more like a party than a trial.

Dawna was asked by her lawyers to keep away from any news related to the trial so her testimony wouldn't be influenced. Sammy and Orlando, however, had been following the trial closely via the Internet and television news. They didn't give Dawna any of the information but dropped hints that it was going well.

When they arrived at the courthouse, Dawna and her aunt went into a special entrance in the back so Dawna would not be intercepted by the hordes of press outside the courthouse. Her Mom, Dad, and Emily were to meet her in a special room where she could wait until it was her turn to testify. She couldn't wait to see her family. It felt like years instead of days since she'd seen them. She hugged Sammy tightly. Then Sammy and Lando left to find their own way into the courtroom.

Dawna was very nervous as Jane, her advocate, led both her and her Aunt Jackie up the back way into the court house. The old building smelled of lemon wax, and the wood floors gleamed. They took a staircase up to the second floor and were led down a hall lined with offices to a room where her parents were waiting. Dawna had never been so glad to see her parents in her life! Well, that wasn't completely true, the night Sammy and her friends returned her home from the kidnappers would definitely trump this day, but still, relief flooded her as her mother and father ran to her side and engulfed her in their arms.

Her parents had left her younger brothers with a family friend, but Emily was in the room, waiting off to the side for her chance to hug her sister. The room held a large wooden table flanked by soft brown leather chairs. They took seats around the table and sipped the ice water provided. There was also a small plate of cookies that looked untouched. Dawna certainly didn't feel like eating, but leaning back in the chair she saw the strained faces of her family staring back at her. Deciding it was time to set them all at ease, she reached forward, grabbed a cookie, and took a huge bite. "Yum, I'm starving," she said through a full mouth.

Emily laughed and grabbed a cookie, "Me too!" She stuffed half the cookie in her mouth.

"You girls!" her mom said shaking her head as she took a cookie.

After that they all seemed to relax a bit and could talk about things going on both at home and at school. They were able to avoid talking about the trial until the door opened and one of the lawyers from the district attorney's office came in to brief Dawna.

The lawyer's name was Leslie Collins and Dawna had met with her once before. She was short and thin, with shoulder length brown hair and huge brown eyes which might have made her look soft, but she wore three inch heels and a black silk suit that gave her an air of stunning professionalism. The way she carried herself made Dawna feel that Leslie Collins was someone she could trust, and she began to relax.

Ms. Collins set her briefcase on the big table and slid into a chair that almost swallowed her. "Let me bring you up to date. We've just finished interviewing the first two girls and their stories line up with everything you have to say, Dawna. Also, the toxicology reports show that all three of you girls were given the same drugs. Frankly, the expert testimonies have helped a lot. As we discussed, the fact that you were drugged for fewer days than the other girls and can give a good description of the men, the van, and the apartment should really lock up this case. You only need to remember to speak clearly so we can hear you and answer honestly as we have practiced. Remember not to answer more than you have to. If we want more detail, we will ask you. Do you have any questions?"

"No," Dawna said, her stomach tightening along with her resolve. "I'm ready to get this over with."

Leslie Collins stood, picking up her briefcase, "Then let's go." She led the way from the room, followed by Dawna, her advocate and the family.

When they got to the courtroom, Dawna's family was led by Jane, the advocate, up to seats near the front, while Dawna was taken by a bailiff to stand off to the side at the right of the room for her swearing in. Dawna cautiously glanced around the full room. She knew Sammy and Lando were sitting a few rows back from her family. She'd snuck a look at them on the way in. To their left, the kidnappers sat with their lawyers. They had chains on their legs to keep them from running away, and they wore bright orange jumpsuits with black bulletproof vests in case an enraged family member of one of the girls tried to shoot them. She could only see their backs as she entered, and was glad for it. Still, a chill ran down her spine knowing she was this close to them again.

A clerk said, "All rise," and everyone stood up as Judge Miller entered the room.

"Prosecution, call your next witness," said Judge Miller looking like Santa Claus seated in a black robe.

Leslie Collins stood to her feet, "Your honor, at this time the prosecution would like to call Dawna J. to the stand." The clerk came over to Dawn and asked her to raise her right hand.

"Dawna J., do you swear to tell the truth, the whole truth and nothing but the truth so help you God?"

"I do," she answered her voice strong and clear.

"You may take the stand."

As Dawna had been instructed, she walked by the jury box and up to sit behind the witness stand. She felt surprisingly calm.

Leslie began her questioning, "Please state your first name and last initial for the record."

Dawna knew they were doing this to protect her identity as a victim. "Dawna J.," she answered.

From this seat she could see the whole courtroom; it was much smaller than she'd anticipated, holding less than a hundred people. Her parents and Emily sat in the front and were all smiling their encouragement to her. A few rows behind them, Sammy and Lando sat looking serious. She drew strength from their presence, focusing on their side of the courtroom, avoiding looking to the right side where the kidnappers sat and, behind them, rows and rows of press people all furiously typing on their laptops.

Ms. Collins approached her, "May I call you Dawna?"

"Yes."

"Now Dawna, do you remember the events that took place June 21st, 2010?"

"Yes."

"Can you tell us, in your own words, what happened that day?"

Dawna began to tell her story, about how she ran away from home to become a model and ended up cold and hungry in Sacramento. There she met the young kidnapper named Chad, who, she found out later, was really named Johnny. The more she talked and answered Ms. Collins' questions, the more confident she felt. After the whole story was told, Ms. Collins asked her the question she'd been dreading.

"Dawna, as you sit in this courtroom today, do you see the men that kidnapped you?"

"Yes."

"Can you please identify them and describe what they are wearing."

Dawna took a deep breath and turned to look at the kidnappers for the first time. Johnny, the younger of the two, was sitting with his head down, not looking at her. But Gary, the big, scary red-bearded man looked her straight in the eye. She felt as if her resolve might slip as he glared at her with hatred.

She glanced at Emily who nodded encouragement. Pointing straight at Gary she declared, "They are sitting right there at the public defenders' table, wearing orange jumpsuits and black, bulletproof vests."

"As you sit here today is there any doubt in your mind that these are the men who kidnapped you?"

"I have no doubt."

"Let the record show the witness has identified the defendants." Ms. Collins turned toward the judge, "I have no further questions, your Honor."

The judge then called the public defenders lawyer to question Dawna.

A tall thin man in a black suit and red tie approached her. His pointed face and slicked back hair reminded her of a weasel.

"Dawna J.," he said as he approached Dawna, "may I also call you Dawna?"

"No," she said, unflinching.

The Public defender almost missed a step at this reply but caught himself and kept going. "I see, Miss J., you said you were drugged when the alleged kidnappers had you, is that correct?"

"Yes."

"If you were drugged, how would it be possible for you to identify the alleged kidnappers?

"I was not drugged when I met Johnny. And who could forget a face like Gary's?"

A chuckle went through the courtroom and Dawna thought she'd even heard it from the jury box.

Nonplussed, the Public Defender continued, now making a point to punctuate the letter J as he spoke, "Miss J., is it true that you ran away from home?"

"Yes, I said that a few minutes ago."

"Well, then tell me this, do normal, happy girls run away from their homes?"

Leslie Collins was on her feet in a flash, "I object you Honor, he is goading my witness."

"Sustained," said Judge Miller. "The public defender will limit himself from questions regarding Miss J's character."

"Of course your Honor, let me rephrase that. Why did you run away from home?"

"As I said earlier, I wanted to be a model."

"And were you unaware that models often end up in professions like stripping or porno films?"

"No,"

"No, you were not unaware?"

Dawna felt panicky. What was he trying to do? Make her out to be some kind of slut? He was twisting her words. She needed to get control of her thoughts. She saw movement in the courtroom behind her. Sammy was sitting up as straight and tall as she could to see Dawna. They locked eyes. Dawna could feel a steely resolve coming to her from Sammy. She answered with confidence.

"No, I did not know that about models. I don't even believe it's true."

The questions went on, but Dawna was back in control now. She answered the best she could with the fewest words and, when the public defender was out of line, Leslie objected quickly.

Relief flooded Dawna as she was finally led down from the witness stand, her legs shaking.

THE DRIVE HOME WAS MUCH more subdued than the ride to Sacramento had been. Dawna was reluctant to say goodbye to her family outside the courtroom as they hugged and cried together. Now she lay curled in the front seat, eyes closed. She could hear Sammy and Orlando going over the trial in soft voices in the back seat. She was too tired to participate but enjoyed listening. For all of Dawna's confident optimism; today drained out all of her energy.

After a while, the tone of the back seat conversation changed. Were they flirting back there? Dawna smiled and let the rhythm of the car lull her to sleep.

CHAPTER TWELVE
TEDDY

ON SATURDAY, TEDDY WOKE UP feeling restless. Emily was suffering over Dawna. He hadn't heard how court went but was afraid to call and ask. Brandi was living through hell with those... weird experiences, and he could do nothing. Finally he decided to do the one thing he could do. He dressed, wearing his warm coat as the weather was cooling significantly. He was going to town. The one thing he could do was try to gather information by touching peoples' skin. He'd never done this intentionally before, but he would today. He'd discovered this ability when he was four. He assumed everyone could do it and used his ability to keep track of how his parents were feeling. But one day his mom had some friends over for a playgroup, and Teddy walked into the kitchen where the ladies were having coffee and announced, "Toby is sad because his dad hit his mom this morning." This caused quite a stir.

Afterwards his mom questioned him at length about his abilities. She taught him he had what she called a "birthright gift."

"Everybody has them," she said. "It's part of being made in the creator's image. It's just that most people don't take the time to notice them." She told him to keep his birthright gift under wraps and not use it to gain information without people's permission, if he could help it.

"Someday you'll know why this was given to you," she assured him.

Today he was going to break that rule. Besides, who could say if this wasn't the very reason he'd been given this gift.

He lived across Highway 49 from Emily, so he was on the right side for heading to town. Getting a ride was easy; the first truck that came by picked him up. He was glad to get inside as he'd forgotten gloves and his hands were starting to hurt in the crisp fall air. Mr. Stevenson gave him a ride in his old white pickup. They sat silently, bouncing along, all the way to town. He felt Mr. Stevenson sneak glances at him occasionally, but he was used to that. He knew he looked different and people couldn't help but stare when they had a chance. He'd spent his life trying to be as invisible as possible and it worked for him, until Emily. Did he wish she'd never asked for a ride to the football game? Not really. He felt he'd been drawn into something bigger now, something meaningful.

He'd noticed people were afraid to touch his extra pale skin, so today was going to be difficult. Teddy ignored the driver's glances and focused on trying to figure out how he was going to gather information. He'd never been the easy extrovert his mother was. The idea of striking up conversations with strangers was painful to him. But, he had to take some risks today; it was the only thing he had to offer. When they reached town Teddy knew it was time, he held out his hand to Mr. Stevenson, who looked confused but shook it anyway.

He felt Mr. Stevenson's intense loneliness surge through him, stunning in its intensity.

Mr. Stevenson suddenly jerked his hand free of Teddy's. He realized he'd held it too long. *Dang, how am I gonna touch folks if I zone out each time?*

"Thank you Mr. Stevenson," he said, wishing he could offer the man more comfort than he could.

The old man nodded before pulling away from the curb.

Teddy stood in the center of town looking around, deciding to start in the bakery. Walking in, he noticed a table full of kids from the middle school. Billy Kip was with the group. His dad and Billy's rode into town together for work. He'd been introduced to Billy more than once but they were not friends. He resolutely walked up to the table and held out his fist to Billy. "Hey Billy," he said.

Billy stopped talking to look up at Teddy. He seemed unsure of what to do, then bumped Teddy's fist lightly. "Hey Teddy," he said, returning the awkward greeting.

Teddy felt sexual energy surge from Billy's fist into his. It snapped him back into the room, his face flushing red, arm still outstretched. Billy looked at him questioningly. He dropped his arm, nodded briefly and walked away from the now confused looking group. *Okay,* he thought, *that was not cool.*

Walking up to the cash register, he ordered a cookie. A pimply faced cashier, her hair held back in a hairnet, handed him the cookie. Their hands brushed and he got another shock of sexual energy that made him feel coated in longing. He left the bakery as fast as he could, breathing hard. This was not going well. He started to doubt the wisdom of his idea. *Is every teenager in this town thinking about sex?* Still, he was already here. He decided to go over to the gas station and see if anyone was hanging around.

The first person he encountered was the town drunk, Guy Dobson. Teddy dug around in his pocket for some change and walked up to Guy. "Here's something for coffee, Mr. Dobson." The bleary eyed man looked him over wearily, finally reaching out for the change. As their hands met, Teddy felt sadness and despair course though his body, and something else—death?

"Move on now, boy." Mr. Dobson said.

He stumbled away. He didn't know if he could take much more of this. Resolutely he turned to go into the small grocery store attached to the gas station. Of the four people inside he'd "accidently" bumped into, two sent stress flowing through his body; they were worried about money. He got nothing from one and the other was thinking about sex.

This is exhausting! He preferred not to know what people in his town were feeling. Discouraged, he decided it was time to hitch a ride back home when he glimpsed the Family Resource Center across the street. They were open on Saturday. He couldn't give up yet! Crossing the street, he walked up to the little white house. He'd never been inside before. The sign said "Come in" so he pushed open the front door as a small bell jangled, announcing his entrance. He stood at the empty counter looking around. The front room held toys and books in a waiting area. A hall led off to his right to other rooms. A white lady came down the hall, a broad smile on her face.

"Hi, I'm Sue!"

"Hi, I'm Teddy." *Now what do I do?* He racked his brain for something to say.

"Um, I was wondering what kind of services you have."

"Oh we have a lot. Are you a local boy? Oh yes, you're Doris' boy aren't you?"

Teddy nodded but Sue wasn't stopping for an answer. He was pretty sure he'd never heard anyone talk as fast as she did.

"Well, you know most of the locals are on welfare or SOS. We've got the ranchers and those like your Daddy that drive up to the lake for work. With all the retirees we have little tax base for education and social services. This town needs all the help we can get. We offer after-school classes, tutoring, counseling and art. It's no wonder that little girl ran away. Did you know her? I guess the trial's over now. Time for the jury to make a decision…"

Teddy's stomach tightened at the mention of Emily's sister. He was beginning to feel a lack of air, as if Sue was using it all up.

"T-That's great," he said jumping in mid-sentence. "Do you have any brochures or anything?"

She stared at him, trying to process his question. "Well, we have a flier here of this month's activities." She pulled a flyer off the stack on the counter and handed it to him.

Teddy took it, turning toward the door. Then, he remembered why he came. Holding out his hand to her he said, "It was nice meeting you, Sue."

"Oh, what a polite young man you are!" She said grasping his hand firmly and shaking.

Teddy was overwhelmed by intense pain. Not from his hand, but from her heart. She was hurting deeply over her daughter, who was about Teddy's age. She was afraid for her and the consequences of the choices she was making. She was devastated. Teddy felt tears constricting his throat.

"Teddy, Teddy, are you okay?" Sue asked frantically.

Teddy shook his head coming back into the room. "Oh, sorry, I zoned out for a minute there."

Sue looked at him, concerned. "You ought to have that checked son. Tell your mom she ought to take you to the doctor. I had a cousin once that kept doing that and it turned out to be epilepsy! She…"

Teddy edged toward the door, opened it and waved goodbye saying "Thanks" as Sue's stream of words followed him out the door.

He'd had enough of his towns' feelings for one day. It was time to look for a ride home.

CHAPTER THIRTEEN
EMILY

MONDAY MORNING, EMILY WALKED down the bus aisle, ignoring all the stares as she headed to her seat. The trial was over and the jury had gone into deliberations. Suddenly, the towns-people seemed much friendlier towards Emily and her family, but she would have none of it. They shunned her family and made life so awful for Dawna she'd had to move to Reno. Did they think Emily would forgive them so fast? She ignored all the eager glances and smiles, sliding into the seat next to Teddy. It felt good to sit next to him; he never changed the way he treated her both before and after Dawna's kidnapping. Quickly she pulled a note from her pocket and passed it to him, hoping no one noticed.

He pulled out his earbuds and took off his sunglasses. The note outlined an early morning call she'd received from Brandi. Brandi's local doctor had referred her to a psychiatrist in Reno. The doctor had a cancelation for tomorrow afternoon, then no openings until January. Brandi's mom agreed to let her drive to Reno herself if she could get a friend to ride with her. Brandi reminded her mom that

Dawna lived in Reno with her aunt. If Emily could go, they might be able to spend the night at Dawna's aunt's home and drive back to Sierraville on Wednesday for school. Brandi's mom reluctantly agreed, but only because weekday mornings were the restaurant's busiest times. Brandi called Emily and asked her several questions, which Emily wrote down for Teddy.

1. Could Emily go with her?

2. Could they stay at her aunt's house?

3. Could Teddy come along so they could do more brainstorming?

4. Could Dawna arrange a meeting with her other "spooky" friends in Reno?

5. Could she please try to keep the whole thing on the "downlow"?

Emily watched Teddy as he read the note a second time. He looked up, "Tomorrow?"

"Yep."

He looked thoughtful. "I'll have to ask my mom, but I don't see why not; I have great attendance. What did your mom say?"

"She was so freaked out by the trial she's glad to let me go there to be with Dawna. She already gave me a note to excuse me from school after lunch."

Teddy glanced back at the note, "So… on the 'down-low,' meaning…she doesn't want us telling any of her friends we're hanging out together, right?"

"I'm sure that's what she means."

Teddy fell silent again, and then he whispered, "How was the trial?"

Emily leaned in toward him to keep anyone else from hearing. "Pretty awful. I'm glad it's over."

"Yeah, I noticed the thaw on the bus."

"Seriously!" she rolled her eyes. "Do they honestly think I'm going to forgive them so easily?"

Teddy smiled slightly, "I guess not. You have a right to be angry. From what I read, it seems like the case is very strong against the kidnappers."

"I hope so. Of the three girls, Dawna actually had the most information. I think because she hadn't been drugged very long before she got rescued. Our lawyer said her testimony really helped pound the nails in the coffin."

"That's good." Teddy fell silent again. Then he changed topics for the third time. "Have you had any more dreams?"

"No, how 'bout you? Feel anything new?"

"Yesterday I hitched into town and went around bumping into people trying to find out some...clue. Instead I got a glimpse into the sick minds of many of our towns' finest."

Emily laughed at the thought of Teddy accidently bumping into people around town. "Yikes! What were they thinking about?"

"Well, I can't read their thoughts exactly, but most I'd say were either thinking about sex or worried about money. Some were really hurting; it was tough."

She noticed the pain etched in his normally tranquil face, "I'm sorry."

The bus arrived in front of the school and the students filed off. The elementary and middle school kids turned to the left and the high schoolers headed to their lockers. Emily opened hers to find a hot pink Post-It that read: "Meet me at the bear, bring T," in Brandi's handwriting.

Emily grabbed Teddy and they headed down the hall to the back entrance of the school where a huge wooden grizzly bear statute stood. Brandi was not there. They circled the bear, nodding at classmates who were streaming in the back door of the school. Then Emily noticed a hot pink paper wedged into the base of the statue. Opening it she saw the words "goat barn."

She and Teddy headed out the back door toward the agricultural classes. The Ag school classes were actually held in barns and fenced areas behind the school. There was one that held goats. They found Brandi standing near the back of the goat barn.

"It's about time you got here, these goats stink!"

"Sorry," said Emily, although she didn't feel very sorry. If Brandi was this embarrassed to be seen with them, she deserved to get her pretty shoes messed up with some goat crap. Emily was starting to feel that this whole "undercover thing" was getting a bit ridiculous.

"What did you want?" she asked irritably.

"Did you find out if you can go with me?" Brandi asked with a tone that implied, *what else could I possibly need to know from you two?* At least that's what it sounded like to Emily.

"I can go, Teddy will ask tonight. Where do you want us to meet you?" Emily was interested in the answer to this question because, meeting at Brandi's car, although the logical place would raise questions among Brandi's friends.

But Brandi had obviously thought this one through, "How 'bout you two head over to the bakery and pick up some goodies for the trip. I'll pick you up there."

Emily shrugged her shoulders, "K." She turned quickly to leave the goat barn but Brandi's voice stopped her.

"Emily, I think Dawna was really brave to testify like that. And, I'm really glad you can go with me. I hope you can go, too, Teddy."

"Me too," said Teddy a little too enthusiastically, which earned him an elbow in the ribs from Emily.

"Ow, what was that for?" he asked as they headed back into the school.

"Don't you understand she's using us? She's all friendly when we're alone and she wants our help, but won't be seen with us in front of her friends. Doesn't that bother you?"

"Well, what else could she do? Don't you think it would draw more attention to her situation if she suddenly started hanging out with two freshmen?"

"Whatever!" Emily said, mad that Teddy defended Brandi.

She pulled open the back door and let it slam in Teddy's face.

CHAPTER FOURTEEN
SAMMY

SAMMY AND DAWNA LAY ON Sammy's bed after school Monday. They were in their usual positions, Dawna propped against the back corner reading, and Sammy on her stomach drawing. Charity was also in her usual place, on the floor beside the bed, coloring.

No one was more shocked than Sammy when Mr. Monahan asked her to make sketch designs for the spring musical, *Man of La-Mancha*. She had never read the play and was surprised to find her face wet when she got to the part where Don Quixote dies. She'd been swept up by the story within a story of the man who'd chased windmills as if they were giants. His ability to see beauty in the town whore, Aldonza, and rename her Dulcinea, or see a golden helmet in a metal pan, moved her deeply. It was a clear example of chivalry and beauty. Sammy hadn't seen much of that in her world. Yet, somehow, it reminded her of last summer, of being on a quest with her friends to help Dawna. Her mind was full of sketch ideas. She was thrilled when Dawna decided to work on the play's costumes.

Sammy had been paying special attention to Dawna's moods since the trial; she noticed now that she was having a hard time concentrating on her book.

"Are you worried about the trial?"

"Yeah," Dawna closed her book with a snap. "Why is it taking so long for the jury to decide? I thought they'd be in an out of their chamber in an hour! It's been three days!"

"Well, really only one, since the trial ended and they didn't go to chambers until Friday."

"Yeah, I guess. I just want to know something!"

"They're probably just trying to be very thorough, so no one can claim they did something wrong."

"You're right Sammy. My lawyer said everybody was minding their p's and q's to make sure no one could ask for a mistrial. It's just hard not knowing."

"Have you allowed yourself to go back and watch any of the coverage on TV?"

"No, I think I'll wait. My aunt Tivo'd everything for me. I can watch it after the verdict."

"Are you going to go to Sacramento to hear the verdict read?"

"No, I don't think so. I don't want to miss any more school, my aunt has to work, and even my parents can't go. No money for gas."

She sounded depressed so Sammy thought she'd change the subject.

"How are the costumes coming for the play?

Dawna's face lit up. "I finished Dulcinea's gown! It turned out great. I'm so excited to be involved in this play. It's fun to have something creative to take my mind off the trial, and my Aunt Jackie has a great sewing machine. How are your sketches coming along? Can I see them yet?"

Sammy wasn't sure she was ready to show her set sketches to anyone, but this was the first time Dawna seemed excited about anything since the trial. She sat up against the wall and opened her art book.

"I haven't shown any of these to Mr. Monahan yet. I know he's getting antsy."

She flipped open to a page and hesitantly pointed to a thin skyline made with a black pencil. In the right corner was the outline of a windmill.

Dawna looked at it thoughtfully. "It's simple, I like it!"

"Really? You don't think it's too simple? It's just that I felt the story was so rich, the background should be, you know, sort of plain in contrast. Like it's almost make-believe, right? More of an idea than an actual place."

"No," said Dawna with enthusiasm, "actually, I think it's perfect. You should definitely show Mr. Monahan. Can I see the rest?"

Sammy relaxed against the wall and turned the page.

"Which scene is this?"

"Uh, no…that's not part of it. It's just a barn I drew." She flipped the page, "this is the scene when Don Quixote knights his sidekick. It's just a barren landscape but I thought it contrasted with the incredible emotion and humor of the scene. You see, I was thinking there could be four cubed flats. Each scene could be on one side, and then they'd just have to turn the cubes once for each scene change. The painted background outlines would go across the flats to form one continuous background."

"Interesting and easy to build, I wonder what Mr. Monahan will say?"

"Me too." Sam flipped to the page. There was another barn.

"What's with the barns?"

"I know, random. I just seem to be drawn to sketching barns lately."

Charity's small head popped up from the floor. "I dreamed about a barn last night."

"You did Itty-Bitty. What did you dream?" asked Sammy. As always, she was surprised Charity was listening to their conversation at all. She needed to be more aware and careful around Charity.

"I dreamed there was a scary barn and little boy was trapped in there. I cried and Mama came and sang to me till I fell asleep."

Sammy felt that old familiar chill run down her spine. This had happened once before, when Charity dreamed of the men in the van who'd captured Dawna. She turned and looked at Dawna who looked as concerned as Sammy felt.

"Charity, did the barn in your dream look anything like this one?" Sammy held the sketch book over the bed so that Charity could see it. Charity leaned over the book, looking intently at the picture.

"Yes, 'cept it was dark inside and Michael was afraid. He wanted his mommy, too!"

"Michael?" asked Dawna.

"That was the boy's name in the dream."

Sam put her hand on Charity's head and stroked her hair. "Itty-Bitty, is there anything else you remember about the dream?"

"Only that it smelled like potatoes." With that her head moved away from Sammy's stroking hand. Charity had gone back to coloring.

"How many barn pictures do you have?" whispered Dawna, a tremble of fear in her voice.

"I'm not sure. I wasn't really even aware I was drawing them. Let's look." They bent their heads over the barn pictures and compared them. There were three of them mixed in among play sketches, and it was obvious that they were all the same barn, but from different angles. The barn was huge and old and mostly falling down. There was one other unexplained drawing, some kind of bar that looked like what you'd hang a towel on. The girls had no idea what to think of it.

"Should we call Emily?" asked Sammy.

"Yeah, but you have no idea how many barns there are like this around Sierraville. They're as common as bus stops are here in Reno."

"Still, we should call."

Just then Dawna's cell phone rang causing both girls to jump and shriek. Dawna clutched her heart, breathing heavily as she answered the phone. She listened carefully,

"Yeah, and what'd they...seriously? Oh my gosh, oh my gosh! Really, to Reno? Sweet!" She started jumping up and down on the bed on her knees. "Okay, goodbye, thanks." She turned to Sammy, beaming, "Guilty on all counts!"

"No way!" said Sammy, jumping to her knees to bounce with Dawna and throwing her arms around her as they jumped their joy. Soon Charity was jumping with them even though she didn't know what they were celebrating.

"Guess what else," asked Dawna?

"What?"

"Emily's coming tomorrow!" she started bouncing again.

CHAPTER FIFTEEN
BRANDI

WHEN BRANDI PULLED UP IN FRONT of the bakery on Tuesday, she was surprised to see Emily head straight for the back seat. Teddy came around to the front, looking concerned as Emily closed the door a little harder than necessary. Teddy looked back at Emily and rolled his eyes before buckling his seatbelt. Brandi thought she knew what might be bothering Emily, but she said nothing. Emily had been mad at her since their meeting in the goat barn and Brandi wasn't sure why, but she imagined it had something to do with the clandestine nature of their friendship. She felt bad about it, but adding one more complication to her life right now would be too much. She thought, *why can't she understand the pressure I'm under?* Frustrated, she pulled out from the curb and headed up the hill toward Reno.

After twenty minutes of stony silence, Brandi decided to try and break the ice. She glanced at Emily in the review mirror. "I'm really glad about the guilty verdicts Emily. That was great news!"

Emily nodded briefly and turned to look out the window.

Brandi looked at Teddy and he shrugged. "So, have either of you had any new information about our "problem?""

Emily's face was like stone. Teddy flipped the visor down to look at her, but she didn't look back. He filled the silence with his story about the trip downtown to accidently-on-purpose bump into people. Brandi kept glancing back at Emily in the rearview mirror, a concerned look on her face. Finally she asked, "Emily, are you okay?"

"Fine," Emily replied shortly.

"You don't seem fine. Have I done something wrong?"

"Well, that depends on a person's perspective," said Emily.

"Um, okay…how about you tell me your perspective?"

Emily sat with her arms crossed tight across her chest, looking out the window. She didn't speak.

Brandi turned to Teddy, "Do you know what I did wrong?"

Teddy looked at Emily in the mirror. She continued to refuse to look at him. "She's upset you only talk to us in private and ignore us at school."

Emily glared at him in the mirror. He shrugged his shoulders as if to say, *what do you want me to do?*

Brandi said, "I wondered if that was it. I'm sorry Emily. I just don't know how to handle what's happening to me. It's not like I'm embarrassed to be your friend or…"

"You could have fooled me," Emily interrupted.

"Well, under normal circumstances, I'd like to hang out with you and Teddy. It's just, well, these aren't normal circumstances. My parents, my teachers and my friends think I'm sick or some kind of freak. They're watching every move I make and I don't want to give them any more ammunition, that's all."

"Yeah, cause if you hung out with us, they'd know you were a freak!"

"That's not what I meant."

"*Whatever.*" Emily turned even further toward the window.

Brandi felt stuck; she looked to Teddy for help.

He said, "Em, we have to focus on the problem at hand. You and I both know that in the normal universe, the three of us would not be hanging out."

Brandi wanted to protest this statement, but didn't because she realized it was true and that grieved her.

Teddy continued, "But for some reason, we've been put together to solve this problem. To rescue this kid trapped in a basement, right? I mean look, it's not by accident you were the one who found Brandi in the bathroom that day. You're the only one who could really understand what was going on with her. Only you knew about how Dawna got rescued, right? It was divine intervention or whatever that brought us all together. And if we have to pretend not to hang out, in order to help whoever is trapped, then that's just part of it."

Brandi realized this was the longest speech she'd ever heard Teddy make. She looked in the rear view mirror to see if it made an impact on Emily's mood. Her face still looked hurt and closed but soon it shifted. Brandi heard Emily sigh.

Finally, she spoke, "Okay, there's something you two should know." Then she told them what Dawna said on the phone about the barns and the boy named Michael.

EMILY COULDN'T BELIEVE IT. Sammy managed to pull Ty, Lando and Tiff together on Tuesday night. That meant the entire Blue

Group would be here. They all met at Aunt Jackie's house. Her aunt seemed excited to be hosting the gathering of friends and very glad to see Emily again. Emily had always been close to her aunt and looked forward to this chance to be with her, even if it was only for a brief time. She wondered why it was easier to talk to her aunt than it was to her mom. Her aunt had graduated from high school and promptly made a beeline to Berkeley for college. This made her seem exotic and interesting to Emily.

Emily's mother married her childhood sweetheart right after high school and never left Sierraville. This was not the kind of predictable future Emily wanted. She thought about travel and going to art school in San Francisco, LA, or maybe even New York. She wanted an interesting life far from her little town.

They enjoyed a great dinner around the table. Once again Teddy talked more than usual and Emily was surprised. At seven o'clock, people began to arrive. First it was Dawna who'd borrowed her aunt's car to go pick up Sammy and Tiff. Emily was very excited to finally meet Tiff in person after hearing so much about her from Dawna. She was a pretty, peppy Korean in sporty clothes. Then the doorbell rang and Ty and Lando walked in. Emily was very interested to meet these two guys who had been so involved in rescuing her sister.

Ty was a tall, handsome African American with a smooth, resonate voice. Lando, who she'd met briefly at the courthouse, was short and stocky with a ready smile. He was charming and extroverted, and seemed particularly attentive to Sammy.

Emily felt awed by their presence because they were older and had risen to larger-than-life proportions in her mind. She was shocked to see Dawna receiving all their hugs and congratulations as if it was normal. Dawna even bantered back and forth with Lando. She watched as they greeted one another warmly and fell into intimate conversations. Emily kept an eye on Tiff and Ty as Dawna had told her about their "almost" relationship last summer. Ty had invited Tiff to his school's homecoming dance but her parents refused to let her go. They said she was too young to date but Tiff was convinced it was also a reaction to Ty's race. He was not even a little bit Korean. Tiff was devastated.

They did seem a little stiff around each other, but Emily wouldn't have noticed if she hadn't been looking for it.

Their aunt made popcorn and cookies and left the eight of them alone together in the living room. Emily wondered if Teddy and Brandi felt as awkward as she did. Neither had said much, although Brandi looked more comfortable than Teddy.

Sammy started the meeting as soon as they were seated. "Well, as I told you, Emily, Brandi and Teddy are going through a similar experience to what we went through last summer. I thought it would be good if Emily would summarize the situation so we could, maybe, offer our advice or ideas." She looked at Emily as if it was the most natural thing in the world for Emily to talk to a room full of juniors and seniors! Emily sat quiet and frozen, but everyone was looking at her and waiting. Finally she realized she had to say something, anything.

"Well, uh, you see, Brandi," she pointed, "she has these…spells." At that moment Emily felt she could see the room from the vantage point of the ceiling. She realized how lame she must look and sound to these people, *just like the country bumpkin I am.* This thought made her sit up straighter, *that is not who I want to be,* she realized.

She started again. "Sammy seems to think we have all been given different gifts which are helping us rescue a boy named Michael. He is trapped in a barn somewhere and we need to find him. The information we have comes from Brandi's experiences of feeling like she *is* the boy; my dreams have me in the basement *with* the boy; and Teddy has the ability to sense and confirm what the two of us are feeling through his hands. The details of the barn and the boy's name came from Sammy's drawings and her little sister...Chasity?" Emily looked at Sammy.

"Charity," Sammy corrected.

"Charity," echoed Emily. "So, that's pretty much all we know. We figured since we had a chance to come to Reno, we might meet with you to get any help or advice you can give us." Emily took a deep breath for the first time since she'd started talking. She realized just how totally crazy all of this sounded when she said it out loud, but none of the people watching her seemed to think it was out of the ordinary. Instead, they were all considering carefully what she said. She let her shoulders drop and began to relax.

Ty was first to speak, "I still can't believe this is happening again. I really thought it was a one-time thing."

Tiff jumped in, "Seriously, me too, I can't get over it."

Lando, who had heard more about it from Sammy during the drive to Sacramento, had an actual question, "Have any of you seen Sammy's barn pictures?"

"Not yet," answered Sammy as she began to pull some sketches from her camo book bag.

"I've taken the three pictures out of my art book so you can see them together." She laid them out side-by-side on the coffee table. The Loyalton high three stood to inspect them.

"Does this barn ring a bell for anyone?" Sammy asked.

All three shook their heads. Teddy explained, "The thing is, there are tons of these old dilapidated barns around the Loyalton area." The other's nodded in agreement.

"Can we take these with us?" Teddy asked. "That way we could, maybe, drive around looking for this specific barn."

"Sure," said Sammy. "There's one other picture, but neither Dawna nor I know what it means or if it's related to the barns." She took the picture of the bar out of the bag and laid it on the table. "Does this mean anything to anyone?"

The three passed the paper between them shaking their heads.

"No clue," said Emily.

"I have a question," said Ty. "I understand how Emily's gift of dreams works, because I share it. But I'd like to hear more about how Brandi's and Teddy's gifts work."

Brandi grimaced, "I sure hate to call what happens to me a gift! It's… terrifying. It's like I'm suddenly myself and somebody else at the same time. Like I feel everything they're feeling and see everything they're seeing. It's horrible."

Ty clarified, "So it's like you're sitting in class and suddenly you're a little boy in a barn?"

"Well, thankfully it hasn't happened in class. But, yeah, it's kinda' like that. It's hard to come out of the, uh, experience of it, too. Like I can't just snap out of it quickly, it takes time. My parents think I'm fainting or something. The psychiatrist I talked to today thinks I'm having stress related seizures. 'Psychogenic Non-Epileptic Seizures' is what he called them. I'd kind of rather believe it was that than what it is, but he wants to put me on some really strong meds. I'm not going to take them either, and I know my folks will have a cow. But first he scheduled me for an MRI. It's really getting out of hand. We need to figure out what's going on. Isn't there any way to speed this up?"

The room fell silent. Finally, Tiff answered, "I'm really sorry, Brandi. We all felt that pressure when we were going through it. We knew we needed to save Dawna but we didn't know how or when. It was really frustrating. But, none of us went through physical torture or anything like you are."

"It's not that bad I guess, I mean, if there is some little boy out there I can help…"

Ty interrupted, his voice serious, "How does your gift work Teddy?"

Teddy seemed startled to be spoken to. He sat still for a moment as if he were trying to understand the question. "I can sometimes feel what others are going through when I touch their skin."

"Seriously?" asked Lando, "That's sick, I wish I could do that."

Tiff laughed, "Wow, Lando, you're learning some slang there."

Lando smiled. "But seriously, just think of how you could do with the ladies if you knew what they were feeling!"

Teddy smiled, sheepishly.

Ty persisted, all business, "But how has this gift helped the… investigation?"

Emily saw how uncomfortable Teddy looked because he was the center of attention. She answered for him, "He was able to confirm, to Brandi and me, that we were experiencing the same thing. And, you know, it could be helpful down the road if he happened to run into the bad guy or something."

Ty nodded, looking thoughtful.

"So do you guys have any ideas for us?" Emily asked hopefully.

The room fell silent again. Then Lando spoke up, "Brandi, do you all live in the same town?"

"No, Teddy and Emily live in Sierraville, we all go to school in Loyalton but I live in Calpine, it's about seven miles from Sierraville. Why do you ask?"

"You should start your search of barns in Calpine."

"How do you know that?"

"I don't know how I know," began Lando and then he was joined by a Blue Group chorus of "I just know!" Then the four laughed.

Tiff was quick to explain, "That's Lando's gift you see. He just *knows* things, sometimes."

"Sick!" said Teddy, surprising everyone. He and Lando exchanged fist bumps and big grins.

Brandi spoke up, "Does anybody have any other ideas?"

Tiff responded, "The most important thing is to keep searching for the answers. You wouldn't have been given this information if you weren't meant to use it for good. It *will* all make sense eventually. You have all been given these gifts for a reason."

"And that's Tiff's gift," said Sammy. "She's like the cheerleader on our team. She encourages us to keep going, and to try new things."

Emily realized she did feel encouraged. She had been feeling like an outsider in her town, in her home, and in her relationship with Brandi. But tonight she felt like she had found a place for herself in a very weird, very unusual group of friends. It felt like a real home.

Now if only there wasn't a boy trapped in a barn.

CHAPTER SIXTEEN
TEDDY

TEDDY WAS DROWSY ON THE WAY back to Sierraville the next morning. They left at six to try and get back on time. He loved every minute of their time with the Blue Group. As they drove, they began to lay out the next steps. They'd stop at the hardware store outside of town and see if they could get area maps. Then, he'd break the areas into three sections and each would drive around comparing the barns they found to Dawna's barn pictures. Even though Lando suggested they stick to the Calpine area, they thought it best to widen the search. Teddy wasn't sure how he and Emily were going to cover their areas because only Brandi had a car.

Then he landed on an idea that might just work.

"Emily and I are both fifteen, old enough to get our driver permits', right?

"Right," said Emily, "But I don't have one, do you?"

"No, but think about it, no one around Sierraville would care if we practice driving around the neighborhoods with our folks. What is there to hit, cows?"

The girls seemed to like this idea. Emily whooped when they pulled into the small hardware store to look for maps. She'd been complaining about wanting a coke for the last half hour.

Hardware is a generous title for this place, thought Teddy. *It's more like a 7-Eleven from the 1800s.*

The store carried a very odd assortment of things travelers and campers might need, plus some old time candies and antique collectibles. The only person in the store was the owner/operator, a tall, bent older man with a fringe of hair around the outside of his head. He didn't seem too happy to see them, as if he didn't trust three teenagers in his store at one time. Brandi headed straight for the restroom and Teddy went to the map section. Emily joined him after getting her soda.

"This is frustrating!" he said.

"What's wrong, Teddy?"

"These maps aren't too great. There are topographic ones, which won't really help for our purposes. There are street maps that are pretty much out of date; they don't even have some of the newer developments. I bet I could find better maps on the internet and print them."

Brandi came up then, waving a long piece of candy in her hand at them, "Look guys, they have Cow Tales!"

Teddy's eyes brightened, "I haven't had one of those since I was a kid. Want one Emily?"

"Sure, but see if they have strawberry. That was my favorite. If not, I'll take chocolate."

Emily filled Brandi in on the map dilemma while Teddy went to find the Cow Tales. He found a chocolate one for him and strawberry for Emily. The old guy behind the counter looked like he'd been sucking on lemons. Teddy handed him a dollar and as their hands touched he felt a rush of cold darkness enter his body. When the girls came up behind him, Teddy was standing at the cash register with two cow tails in his hand and a faraway look in his eyes. The owner, who had just handed Teddy his change, was staring at him with a frown on his face.

Emily bumped Teddy as she came up to the counter, taking the cowtail from his hand. "Teddy, you found strawberry!"

He shook his head, coming fully back into the room and shivering. Emily pushed him toward the door while saying "thanks" over her shoulder to the man behind the counter. Brandi followed close behind them looking worried.

When they got in the car Brandi turned to the back to face Emily, "What was that about?'

"Maybe we should ask Teddy, he's the one that went into zombie mode in there."

Teddy was chewing on his lower lip, looking thoughtful. "It's just, when that guy handed me my change, I got this awful creepy feeling."

"Like what kind of feeling?" asked Brandi.

"I can only describe it as just dark, cold and evil."

Emily shivered, "There's no barn around here. The only other car here is that rusty old Cadillac." Teddy saw a beat-up, faded blue Caddy parked by the left side of the store.

"I am totally creeped out," said Brandi, backing the car out of the parking lot.

"Me too," said Teddy.

"Me three," said Emily. They sat in silence as Brandi drove, finally Emily spoke, "Okay, obviously there is nothing we can do about this right now."

"What do you mean?" asked Teddy. "This could be the guy. We should go back there and not let him out of our sight. We should follow him home. Maybe he'll lead us to the barn."

"Guys, I hate to break it to you," said Brandi, "but I promised my mom I'd be back in school as soon as we got back. We can't just wait here for something to happen."

Teddy felt desperate; this guy was definitely bad news!

Emily interrupted his thoughts, "Teddy, we don't know for sure he's our guy. We only know you felt something evil. He could just be some other dude with an evil vibe."

"Great," said Teddy.

"Really, we don't know Teddy. We can't just accuse him. I have an idea. You do the thing with the maps. I'll ask my dad if he knows anything about that guy at the store. My dad knows everybody in Sierraville. Then, you and I have to ask our parents to take us out for driving practice. Then, we'll call each other tonight and give updates, all right?"

Brandi nodded, "I'll ask my mom, too. She knows most of the folks around here 'cause they all stop at the restaurant."

Teddy agreed, "I'll ask my mom too. But I hate to leave that guy. What if he is *the* guy?"

Emily agreed, "I know Teddy, I hate it too, but we don't really have any choice right now. Teddy looked back at the hardware store as they left it in the dust.

CHAPTER SEVENTEEN
EMILY

EMILY DROVE HER DAD CRAZY until he agreed to take her driving Wednesday night. He tried resisting the adventure on the grounds of having no money for gas, but she produced the twenty dollars her Aunt Jackie slipped to her during her Reno visit, so he had no other argument. She was a bit disappointed he'd caved so easily. She'd been ready to pull the neglected middle child ploy.

Emily remembered when Dawna was learning to drive, "Don't drive with Dad!" she'd said. "He's a nervous wreck! Ask Mom to go, she's much calmer."

But it was Dad Emily needed to question, so she asked him instead. Dawna was right. Driving with her father was turning out to be harder than it sounded. He was very nervous and she'd never driven before. She had to keep focusing on which was the brake, and the gas, then the clutch.

After five failed attempts to get his truck out of the driveway, she talked him into letting her drive her mom's car with an automatic transmission instead. After that, things went more smoothly.

Although she didn't have a map from Teddy yet, he told her he had given her Sierraville and Loyalton and she pretty much knew what that meant. As they were driving, in the long stretch between the two towns, Emily noted three large abandoned barns. None of them looked exactly like the one in the drawings. They talked about Thanksgiving the next day and how glad they were that Dawna was coming home. He asked her what she knew about Sammy and Lando, who were coming with her, and why they wouldn't be with their own families for the holiday? She answered the best she could, "Dawna says Sammy's folks work overtime on the holiday and celebrate on Saturday. She said Lando's folks don't celebrate Thanksgiving because it's about land being taken from the indigenous peoples."

"Is he Indian?" her dad asked.

"No, he's from El Salvador. I'm not sure what the connection means."

"Well, they had a similar problem in El Salvador," her father informed her. "Quite a big civil war if I remember correctly."

She kept her father busy by asking questions about the barns: who they belonged to and why they were so run down. She was amazed at her father's extensive knowledge of people who lived in the area. It was then she decided to bring up the man at the hardware store.

"Hey Daddy, do you know that guy who runs the hardware store outside of town?"

"You mean the one up 89?"

"Yeah."

"Why do you ask?"

"We stopped there the other day, on the way home from Reno. I was just wondering about him."

"That's Frank Riley. He's been in town about three years. Said he came here to retire but decided to buy the hardware store when John Tompkins died. He's made some good changes to it, too."

"Like what?"

"Well, nothing I'd buy, mind you, but like putting in those antiques and the old fashioned candy. Those were his ideas, says he likes the olden days and collects antiques out of the abandoned barns in the area."

Emily jerked the wheel so hard she almost drove into a ditch.

"Emily Louise Jensen, you scared the piss out of me! I think that's enough driving for one day! Pull over and trade me places."

Emily didn't mind switching with her father.

Her hands were shaking too much to drive anymore.

CHAPTER EIGHTEEN
SAMMY

SAMMY SMILED AS SHE PACKED an overnight bag. The idea sprung up suddenly but within hours everything was confirmed. Dawna invited Sammy and Lando to go to Sierraville for Thanksgiving. Her mom said yes, and she even offered to bake some cookies to take with them. Lando's Mom was thrilled he was making friends and immediately said yes to the trip. The only problem was Charity, who would watch her? Then thoughtful Dawna suggested they bring her along. She said Charity could play with her little brothers and her mom would be happy having a house full of people.

Sammy grinned because her life had changed so much in the last six months. She'd never been this happy before. She had friends and was working on the play at school and, possibly, could she even allow herself to think it... a boyfriend? She and Lando hadn't ever said the words out loud but he had been calling her more often and Facebooking her almost daily. She was starting to wonder if they were becoming "something." This weekend she hoped to get more of an idea where they stood. The thought made her stomach squeeze with nerves. Of course, Dawna said it was obvious Lando liked Sammy. She sure hoped Dawna was right!

There was a knock on the front door as Sammy quickly zipped up her suitcase. Charity was beside herself, jumping up and down with happiness. This was her first road trip without her mother, and she felt very grown up. Sammy opened the door to find Dawna smiling like Alice in Wonderland's Cheshire Cat. "My uncle drove his new Esclade!"

"What's that?" Sammy stooped to pick up Charity's suitcase, turnoff the lights and check the apartment one last time.

"Wait till you see. It's like riding in a limo! Each section has its own radio controls, heat and air-conditioning. There's even a movie player. We brought a Disney movie in case Charity gets bored."

Lando's smiling face radiated joy as he jumped out of the Esclade to hold the door open for Sammy. "Wait till you see inside this car!" he said, grabbing her bags to put in the back. He helped Charity get in and then Sammy climbed in. Charity sat on the captain's seat in the second row of seats so she could see the DVD, and Dawna sat next to her. Sammy wondered if she'd done this on purpose to make sure she and Lando sat together in back. She noticed Dawna's sly smile and gave her one in return before she crawled back to the bench seat. Lando immediately started pointing out all the cool features in the car to Sammy who was duly impressed.

They all chatted happily for a while. Charity settled down to her movie and Dawna plugged in headphones. Sammy suddenly felt nervous as she and Lando were virtually alone together. Thankfully, Lando, as usual, quickly made her feel at home – telling amusing stories about his debate team and how his grades were improving.

Lando was even considering a run for a class office next year. Sammy was amazed; his life had changed as much in the last six months as hers.

Suddenly Lando got serious, "Sammy," he began tentatively. "There's something I've wanted to ask you."

She felt her throat constrict. She hoped whatever it was; she could answer with a nod or a shake because she didn't think her voice would work right now.

"I was wondering if you would go with me to my school's home-coming dance in December."

This was not anything Sammy had anticipated. Her, go to a dance? The idea seemed ludicrous. This thought must have showed on her face because Lando started back peddling,

"I mean if you don't want to, that's okay. I just thought maybe it would be nice…" His voice trailed off and he looked miserable.

Sammy knew she needed to say something quickly.

"Lando, I don't really know how to dance."

"Oh," he smiled broadly, "That's no problem, I can dance good enough for both of us!"

She smiled. She was sure this was true. She would go to the dance and she would enjoy watching Lando as he danced "good enough for both of them."

CHAPTER NINETEEN
EMILY

THE TURKEY WAS EATEN, the pies too, and everyone was settling down around the house, full and happy. Emily, Dawna, Sammy and Lando were locked in a deadly battle of Monopoly while Charity and the boys whooped and ran circles around the room. The phone rang and Emily, who had just lost all her property to Lando, jumped up to get it.

It was Brandy, her voice low as if she was sneaking the call.

"I think I found the barn."

"Really?"

"Yeah, but I can't get away until tomorrow. Can I pick you up in the morning?"

"Sure. Dawna, Sammy and Lando are here, can they come?"

"Yes, and I'll get Teddy."

"AT TEN O'CLOCK FRIDAY MORNING Brandi rolled up in her mom's Suburban. Teddy, who sat on the front bench seat, scooted over to make room when Emily climbed in next to him. Dawna,

Sammy and Lando piled eagerly into the back, excited to be part of the search.

"How'd you find it?" Emily asked when they were all settled.

"I ran to the store Wednesday night – Mom forgot one of her spices for pumpkin pie. I took a short cut home and noticed it, even though I've probably seen it a million times. Then we left yesterday morning for my aunt's in Sacramento and didn't get back until I called you.

"You sure it's the right barn?" asked Lando.

"*Not* a hundred percent, but as best as I could compare it to the picture in the dark, it looked right, and it's in Calpine, like you said."

Emily enjoyed the scenery as they drove the winding seven miles west from Sierraville to Calpine. The houses became nicer and were better cared for. The road twisted through beautiful woods and occasionally they'd glimpse a river or stream. She noticed the mood in the car was light, as if they were going on an adventure together. It felt much better with six kids, not just the three of them. Somehow, having the Reno contingent made Emily feel safer. As if together they were invincible.

Brandi's voice broke into her thoughts, "It's coming up around this next corner."

The talking stopped when the barn came into full view. Emily could hear their breathing. She held up the picture of the barn and everyone leaned in for a closer look, glancing from the drawing to the barn in front of them.

"Yep," said Sammy. "That looks like it to me."

"What should we do now?" asked Teddy.

Brandi pulled her car onto a wide spot and turned off the ignition. The only sound was the engine ticking as it cooled.

Brandi spoke, "The barn is abandoned but it's still private property. See the fence?"

Emily glanced at the faces around her. Sliding the drawings onto the dash, she cleared her throat, "Well – Michael isn't going to be rescued with us sitting out here." She opened the door, sliding her feet to the ground and heading for the fence. Five bodies piled out to follow her.

"Wait up," said Teddy, walking fast to catch up with her.

They found a place in the fence where the barbed wire was loose enough to push down and step through. Teddy held it down until everyone was over. They hiked across the dirt lot toward the barn.

Dawna caught up with Emily and whispered, "What's gotten into you, sis?"

"What do you mean?"

"It's just that you're so brave now. When did that happen?"

"I don't know. I just want Brandi to be okay, and that little boy to be safe and if that means going into this barn, well…then we need to do it."

Dawna looked at her sister intently before smiling, "Right, whoever you are, lead on."

Emily rolled her eyes and focused on the barn. Why *was* she being so brave? This was definitely not her normal self. Reaching the side of the barn, she stopped and gestured for the rest of them to line up behind her. Walking slowly and quietly up to a corner of the barn, she took a deep breath before peeking around the front. Nothing. There were no cars parked in front of the barn. She led the group forward. Around the corner Emily could see the entrance had fallen in and was leaning quite a bit to the right.

"This place may not be safe to go into. Maybe I should just check it out."

"No way," said Teddy and Dawna together.

"I think we should all go," suggested Lando.

They tiptoed into the dark barn – stopping until their eyes adjusted. The barn was empty except for an old hay bale stacked against the left side.

"That hay might be all that's holding this thing up," Emily whispered. "Does anyone have a flashlight?"

"I've got one on my keychain," Brandi whispered back, pushing the bottom of the small flashlight and handing it to Emily.

"Dang, that's bright," said Lando.

"LED," Brandi explained.

Emily walked toward the back of the barn, shining the light. It was then she saw it, a door set into the floor.

"Do barns even have basements?" asked Lando.

"Root cellars," Teddy whispered as he slipped in to stand at Emily's side.

Emily felt her stomach lurch. In her dream the bad person was coming down the stairs. The last thing she wanted to do was go down to that awful place. But, if little Michael was down there, she knew she had to do it.

"Teddy, help me open the door. Brandi, hold the flashlight."

She and Teddy grabbed hold of the large wooden door handle and pulled. It opened very easily and silently on well-oiled hinges, which Emily found disturbing in the dilapidated barn. Listening at the opening, the group inched close but heard nothing. Emily took the flashlight from Brandi and shined it downward where steps lead into the root cellar.

"It looks like a small space," Dawna whispered. Her nose twisting at the smells wafting up from below, "We'd better keep a lookout up here, but you yell if you get into trouble down there."

Emily nodded, taking her first tentative step down. She was almost knocked the rest of the way down when Teddy rushed to join her. He stood so close behind her she could feel his breath on the top of her hair. She swung the flashlight back and forth in wide arches until it reached the back wall of the room. She froze. There it was: the pile of rags on the ground near the wall. It was not moving, were they too late?

As the light hit the rags she saw them move and choked back a scream. Had they really moved? The light was shaking in her trembling hand, so she couldn't be sure if the rags had really moved. She had to get closer.

"What's happening?" whispered Brandi urgently from above.

"Rags," Emily whispered back and heard Brandi gasp.

Emily moved slowly down the steps, Teddy was on her heels with Brandi coming down the stairs behind him. When Emily was convinced no boogiemen lurked in the cellar, she gingerly stepped onto the floor. Soon the three stood side-by-side filling the width of the little room. They slowly approached the bundle of rags. Suddenly, something made a rustling sound near Brandi who practically jumped into Teddy's arms. Two eyes glowed at them in the dark.

Was someone standing there? A child?

Emily raised the shaking light toward the glowing eyes. A large rat fled from the top of an old barrel of potatoes. Emily exhaled in surprise; unaware she'd been holding her breath. Turning back to the rags, she was close enough to kick them. Tentatively, she reached out her toe, pulling a rag toward her. It came away, revealing more old potato sacks underneath. Teddy leaned down and whispered for Emily to shine the light closer. He reached in and started pulling the rags apart, until there was only dirt. Nothing, there was nothing there at all. Emily was instantly relieved. She aimed the flashlight into every corner of the room just to be sure, but there was no one.

"What's this?" asked Teddy leaning closer to the pile of rags. Emily handed the light to him. It illuminated a bar, like a pull-up bar mounted onto the back wall of the barn near the rags. The bar was shiny and new and looked completely out of place in the old barn. "I don't know what this is, but it sure doesn't belong here," he said. Brandi gasped, "Teddy, it's the bar from the picture. Which means this is the right barn."

"But there's no Michael," said Emily. They stood in stunned silence.

Lando's voice from above them broke in, "What's happening down there?"

Teddy answered, "There's nothing here."

Brandi whispered. "Let's get out of here; this place is giving me the creeps!"

They turned as one and headed up the stairs, glad for the relative light and fresher air of the barn.

"Find anything?" asked Dawna.

"Nothing human anyway," said Emily. "There was a bar on the wall down there, Sammy, like your picture!"

Sammy's eyes got huge, "No way!"

"Yep," said Teddy, "Shiny and new."

"What do you think it means?" asked Sammy.

"Hey you guys," Brandi cut in. "My house is only a few blocks away. Do you want to come over? We can talk about it there. It's cold here, and we have leftover pie."

"Pie," said Lando.

"Pie," echoed Teddy.

Emily exclaimed in disbelief, "How you guys can be hungry after this is beyond me!"

THAT NIGHT, EMILY SNUGGLED into bed next to Dawna and re- alized she felt perfectly content. It was so good to have Dawna home, even if she had to leave in the morning. She found comfort in the gentle breathing sounds of Sammy and Charity sleeping in Dawna's old bed. She loved knowing that Lando was asleep on the couch and her parents were happy. Her house and her heart were full.

Hanging out at Brandi's house had been fun. After the stress of the barn, her big beautiful house was warm and inviting. Her moth- er, who had closed the restaurant for the holiday, was more than happy to pull out leftover pie and ice-cream, stuffing their already full tummies'. They talked and laughed and played games until they knew they'd better get home before their folks could feel gypped out of their visit with Dawna.

Of course there was the unresolved issue of the boy named Mi- chael kept in the barn, but he wasn't there today. Maybe he didn't even exist. She pushed the thought of him to the back of her mind, turning over, facing her sister with a smile.

She felt happy for the first time in a long time.

CHAPTER TWENTY
Sammy

SAMMY AND DAWNA LEFT MCQUEEN'S Theater after a meeting with the tech team. Sammy was glowing. Mr. Monahan loved her ideas for the set design and the stage crew had already begun work on the four-sided set pieces. Mr. Monahan wanted six of them instead of four, and today they could begin to see what it would look like.

"I love it!" Dawna said.

"Me too."

"What's it like to have something you came up with begin to take shape before your eyes?"

"I don't know. I guess it's like when I draw, but on a bigger scale and so exposed – it's out there for everyone to see, which is kind of intimidating! But I really like how it is shaping up. I think it will work."

"I think it's like when I sew. I love to see the dresses for Dulcinea emerging out of the fabric like magic. I love being a part of creating something from start to finish."

The girls talked as they walked up the hill to Sammy's apartment, stopping to pick up Charity at the neighbor's house on the way. As usual, Charity was a chatterbox, spewing a steady stream of stories about school as they climbed the steps to the front door.

"…and Jimmy, he spit! He actually spit in the classroom, and Mrs. Taylor sent him right to the office. I'm glad because he is always pinching me and I hate it."

The house phone was ringing when Sammy unlocked the door. Charity raced past to grab for the phone, but quickly turned to Sammy, holding it out. "It's your boy-frrriend," she said, drawing out the last word.

Sammy turned to Dawna and smiled, a faint blush coloring her pale cheeks as she took the phone.

"Hi, Lando."

"Glad you knew who Charity meant."

Sammy could hear the smile in his voice and her heart warmed. "Who else would it be?" she teased.

"Hey, I'd love to chat but I have something serious to tell you."

Sammy held her breath. Was he going to break up with her? They had barely started dating, if you could call holding hands on the way back from Sierraville dating.

"What's up?" she said evenly.

"I just started having one of those strong feelings about the kid-in-the-barn thing."

Sammy felt relief flood her quickly followed by guilt. The boy in the barn was more important than her dating life! What was wrong with her? Her emotions were riding a roller coaster lately.

"What does it mean, Lando, what should I do?"

"Well, do you have a number to get a hold of Emily? I feel like something is going to happen today and I need to warn them."

Sammy glanced at the kitchen clock, it was three-thirty. She held her hand over the receiver and talked to Dawna.

"Do you have a way to reach Emily? Lando needs to tell her something."

"She should be home by now, I'll try calling."

Dawna pulled out her cell phone and punched the speed dial number for home. Sammy watched, filling Lando in on what was happening. Soon Dawna hung up.

"She's not back yet. Mom said she called and said she was staying after school and had a ride home. She doesn't have a cell, but I can track down Brandi's number. Just give me a few minutes."

Dawna sat on the recliner near the window dialing friends. Sammy turned back to her phone conversation.

"Lando, how do you get these 'knowings'?"

"I don't know, Sammy. They just come on me sometimes. I don't get them very often. But let me tell you what you need to say. First, I just feel strongly that today is the day. Second, tell them to be careful. Third, and well, this is actually just for you: I think you're really pretty."

Sam felt her face flush with warmth.

CHAPTER TWENTY-ONE
EMILY

EMILY AND TEDDY WERE AT their lockers after school Monday, and Brandi was standing in a crowd of her popular friends. Suddenly, she said good-bye to her friends and came over to join Emily and Teddy. She asked if they wanted a ride home and said it loud enough for her whole posse to hear. Emily glanced at Teddy, who nodded slightly and they left the building, leaving behind a wake of shocked cheerleaders.

As soon as the car doors shut, Emily began her questions.

"What was that about? What brought this on?"

Brandi smiled sheepishly. "I'm sorry it took so long guys. I just realized you're my friends. I enjoy being with you and I don't want to hide it anymore. Do you wanna go to the bakery?"

"Wow, this is serious," said Emily. The bakery was where all the students went after school, not that there were many options. But it would be a very public place to hang out together, that's for sure.

At the bakery they each ordered one of Vicky's amazing brownies.

"You should have seen your friends faces when you walked over to us." Emily said for the third time. "It was like they went from curiosity, to shock, to disbelief." She was interrupted by Brandi's ringing cell phone.

Brandi listened, and mouthed "your sister" to Emily. Emily turned to Teddy and they both shrugged.

Brandi said, "Okay, uh-huh. That's it? Okay, thanks, Dawna. Yeah, we'll let you know as soon as…we know anything. Tell Lando thanks. Bye."

Emily was starring holes in Brandi waiting to hear what had been said. She put the phone away and leaned across the table so they could hear her lowered voice.

"Dawna said that Lando just called. He's had one of his 'knowings.'"

"What's a *knowing* again?" asked Emily.

"Well, he gets them, like when he told us the barn was in Calpine, and he was right. Anyway, he had two things to say. One, he thinks today is the day for the boy in the barn."

Emily felt like ice water had just been poured down her shirt. She shivered, and was surprised when Teddy grabbed her hand under the table. Her head jerked backwards and he quickly dropped her hand.

"What was the second thing?" he asked.

"He said to be careful."

"*That's it?*" asked Emily. "Did he give any details? Where are we supposed to go? What are we supposed to do? What time will this happen?"

"Nope, that was all," she said quietly.

"Great," Emily sighed, looking down at her half eaten brownie, suddenly not hungry. "Well, maybe we should, ya know, drive to the barn then."

Brandi and Teddy nodded grimly, pulling back their chairs.

"You gonna eat that?" asked Teddy pointing to Emily's leftover brownie.

"No, go ahead."

He grabbed a napkin and wrapped the brownie, shoving the treasure into his pocket as they walked to Brandi's car. Snow that had started falling while they were inside was now coming down in heavy wet flakes.

Buckling in, Brandi asked, "Do you think we should call the sheriff?" They sat quietly thinking. "I guess that wouldn't really make sense would it?" she added.

"Not yet," Teddy commiserated. "But if we get there, and find something, we'll call then."

Emily laughed, "Wouldn't that give old Terberg a jolt?" She didn't like Sheriff Terberg much after he questioned Dawna the morning she returned home. He had not been gentle with her.

"He might have to get off his donut-loving butt and do something." Emily laughed at her own joke, but knew it was nervous laughter. *What's wrong with me? I need to get a grip.*

Brandi pulled the car onto the road and headed up the hill toward the turnoff for Calpine. Snow was starting to stick on the roads and Emily was thankful for the four-wheel drive. They were on the turnoff road five minutes when they noticed an old beat-up Cadillac pulling out of a side road a ways ahead of them.

"Hey guys," said Teddy, leaning forward between the seats. "Is that the Caddy from that hardware store?" Emily leaned up to the windshield squinting to see through the snow.

"It could be. Was that one blue? I think this one is, or used to be blue."

"Yeah, it was blue."

Emily took a deep breath.

"Well what should I do?" asked Brandi, her voice rising in panic. "Should I speed up and catch up with him or what?"

"No," Teddy cautioned. "Stay back, just keep him in sight. Let's just see what he does."

As they continued driving, the road became curvier. They lost sight of the Caddy several times, but would round a curve and see it again. Once, after losing sight, they came around a corner and saw the car stopped on the road ahead. Brandi instinctively slowed down.

"What's he doing?" she asked.

Emily leaned forward again, straining to see through the thickening snow. "He's talking to someone on the side of the road. He's opening the passenger door." Emily slammed back against her seat, her breath coming out in a rush. "It's a kid. He just got a kid into his car! What if it's Michael?"

Brandi said, "No, Michael must already be in the barn. Remember how I was Michael and I was already there. Maybe he's taking another kid! Or maybe there are two barns, we didn't even think of that. What if Michael's been in the other barn all along?"

"He's going faster," Teddy noted. "We should call the sheriff now, right?"

"I don't know," Emily hesitated. "It's not like he pulled the kid into that car, maybe he just offered him a ride home so he wouldn't have to walk in the snow. What if he knows him or something?"

Brandi accelerated to close the widening gap between her car and the Caddy.

Teddy argued, "But we know this guy is shady. I could feel that when I touched him, and he's driving toward the barn."

"He's driving to Calpine, just like we are. Maybe he lives over there," said Emily. She looked at Brandi's tense face, her hands gripping the steering wheel, and then at Teddy, who was even paler than usual.

"Okay, here's the plan," she said. "We follow him and if he takes the side road that leads to the barn, then we call the sheriff. Okay?"

"Okay," Teddy whispered. Brandi nodded, her eyes focused on the road which was becoming slippery in the snow.

A mile later, the Caddy turned off on the road that led toward the barn.

"Oh no, oh no, oh no!" Emily cringed. "He's heading for the barn! Okay, Brandi, give me your phone." Brandi dug her cell out of her pocket and handed it to Emily, who punched in 911, but there was no sound.

"No signal, we have no signal!"

"Shit," Brandi spit. "This is a dead area. There is a signal closer to my house, but I always drop calls over here. What should we do?"

"Okay," said Emily. "Listen, we follow him to see if he goes to the barn. Then, if he does, you drop us off where we crossed the fence last time, and drive to an area with cell service and make the call."

"Well, what are you going to do?" asked Brandi.

"I don't know. But we just can't let that little boy get hurt. Oh, I'm so stupid. I should have let you call the Sheriff earlier. I'll kill myself if he gets hurt because of me."

"No," Teddy admonished. "Don't talk like that. You were right, we don't know for sure. Let's just stay focused."

Brandi pulled the car off the road where they had parked before. They stared across the field trying to see if the Caddy had taken the road around into the barn. "There it is," Brandi said, pointing to a spray of mud that was flying up toward the front of the barn. Emily opened the door and jumped out followed quickly by Teddy.

"Go Brandi!"

As Teddy and Emily raced for the fence, they could hear Brandi's car driving up the road. Crouching low, they ran across the field toward the side of the barn. By the time they reached the barn, they were both breathing hard. Leaning their backs against the wall for shelter from the falling snow, they struggled to catch their breath.

"Listen," whispered Teddy.

Emily listened and could hear the door to the root cellar being opened. Her heart was beating so fast she thought it would burst from her chest. When she heard a high-pitched voice cry out, she started running with Teddy close on her heels. As they rounded the corner they could see the Cadillac, white from a dusting of snow. Teddy grabbed Emily's arm, stopping her from racing into the barn. He pulled her close and whispered into her ear.

"Let's go in quietly," he said. She nodded.

They entered the blackness of the barn and waited for their eyes to adjust. When the outline of the room became visible, they tiptoed to the root cellar and saw the door wide open, resting on the barn floor. Kneeling close, they listened. Emily could hear the clinking of metal and a child's voice crying softly. She looked around for any kind of weapon but saw nothing. She knew they were heading into a trap. What if the guy had a gun? What if he heard them coming and hit them with a shovel or something?

Still, she could not leave little Michael. She stood, preparing to storm down the steps, but Teddy grabbed her trying to push past her. He almost succeeded but she was small and fast, and slipped around him barreling down the steps into the pitch pitch-black room. She couldn't see anything except a spot on the barn wall illuminated by a flashlight. Crying was coming from directly in front of her. She stumbled towards the sound. Suddenly, she ran smack into the man who had turned to face her. It felt like she slammed into a brick wall. The air left her lungs in a whoosh and she collapsed onto the man.

"What the hell?" the man shouted as he tried to untangle her from his body.

Teddy rushed down the stairs behind her shouting, "Get away from her, mister," his feet left the bottom step and leaped forward.

The man, whose eyes were accustomed to the darkness, grabbed Emily by the arms and threw her against Teddy as he approached. Teddy was slammed hard against a wooden beam, with the force of Emily's body crashing into him. Teddy's head made a thudding sound against the wood and a groan escape his lips as he slid to the dirt, pulling Emily with him. The man bolted around them, heading for the stairs.

Emily jumped to her feet, then hesitated, "Teddy?"

"Get him," Teddy moaned.

Emily dashed up the stairs behind the man and lunged for his leg as it hit the top of the stair. Grabbing his pant leg, she caused him to lose his balance and fly forward onto the barn floor. Scrambling out of the root cellar, Emily dove on top of the man's back without thinking. He smelled of cigar smoke and peppermint and he started squirming to get away from her. His chest was heaving but his elbow punched back into her ribs. Pain exploded in her side as it connected.

The sudden shock of pain caused her to lose her hold on him and he rolled sideways, knocking her back to the floor. Clawing at the ground, he was trying to get his legs under him when Teddy's head, now dripping blood, popped over the top of the stairs. The man regained his footing and ran, stumbling from the barn. Teddy surged from the stairwell and ran to cover the ground between them. He flew through the air like a tight end, hitting the man from behind as he reached the open air at the front of the barn. The man was flailing under him and Emily could see the blood on the back of Teddy's head dripping onto the man below him.

Teddy looked up at her as she raced to his side, "Help me."

Emily wasn't sure what to do. She ran over and knelt on the man's legs so Teddy could concentrate on keeping his upper body pinned. Then Emily heard a car and looked up to see Brandi driving fast up the driveway. She jumped out of the car and ran to them.

"Do you have any rope?" yelled Teddy.

Brandi ran back to the car and dug around in the back. She returned with a pair of jumper cables. "This is all I could find." She handed them to Teddy who wrestled the man's arms behind his back and tied them as best he could with the cables.

"The sheriff is coming," said Brandi. "Was he down there? Michael? Was there more than one boy?"

Emily felt stricken; she'd momentarily forgotten the boy while dealing with the man. "We didn't see him but we heard him. I don't know if there are more boys down there than the one we saw on the road."

Teddy flipped the man over and Emily could see that it was Frank Riley from the hardware store. His hair was a mess and he looked very angry. Teddy dragged him back into the barn and pushed him to sit against the inside wall of the barn, out of the snow.

"Brandi," Emily said, "Let me have your flashlight; I need to get down there. The poor kid is probably freaking out."

"I want to go, too," Brandi pleaded. "I felt like I *was* him, ya know."

Emily looked at Teddy, "You gonna be okay out here alone?"

Teddy glared down at Mr. Riley whose shoulders now drooped, his head hanging down. The fight had gone out of him. Teddy rubbed his hand over his hair and came away with bloody fingers. He asked Brandi, "You have anything in your car I could bash his head in with if he tries to run?"

Brandi ran to the car and came back with a car jack and her cheer sweater, "This work?"

"That's perfect, but what's the sweater for?"

"Your head! You need to stop that bleeding."

Teddy shrugged and held the letter sweater to his dripping wound.

Brandi and Emily turned to go and Teddy stopped them.

"Wait up, Emily, the brownie in my pocket – he might be hungry."

Emily reached into Teddy's pocket, removing a slightly smashed napkin wrapped brownie from the bakery.

Emily and Brandy hurried to the stairs and slowly down into the cellar. Brandi shined her flashlight to the back of the room where they could see a pile of rags moving by the wall. Emily could hear a soft whimpering sound. She said, "Michael, is that you?"

The whimpering stopped and the rag pile was still. They slowly crept closer as Emily talked. "Michael, my name is Emily and I'm here with Brandi. We are here to help you. Are you okay?"

"Yes," a small voice answered shakily.

"Can you come to us?" she asked.

"I can't," he explained, "My hand is stuck."

"Are you alone down here? Are there any other kids?"

"I don't think so."

The girls moved in and knelt down near the pile of rags. Brandi flashed her light on Emily's face and then on her own. "We are here to help you Michael – the bad man that took you is all tied up. The sheriff is on his way and he will be able to help us get you out of here. Can you sit up at all?"

Brandi handed the flashlight to Emily who aimed the beam on Michael. All they could see was a disembodied arm, attached by a handcuff to the pull-up bar. The rest looked like a pile of rags. He began pushing off the potato sacks and trying to sit up. Brandi moved closer and helped him until he was sitting against the cellar wall, his arm attached to the pull-up bar. He was alone.

Michael was little, about seven-years-old, and missing his two front teeth. He looked small and frightened. He was about Parker's size Emily realized; tears started falling as she felt the pain and injustice of what had happened to him. The realization hit her that it could have been so much worse. It was like Dawna, rescued before she had been raped, a miracle. Michael was shaken but he would be okay. Grace.

Brandi gently offered the brownie to the scared boy, "Are you hungry? We have a brownie here if you are." He hesitantly took the brownie with his free hand and nibbled off a small bite. Emily saw a tentative smile on his pale face.

"Will you be okay down here with Michael? I want to go check on Teddy."

Brandi ruffled Michael's hair, "Sure, we'll be all right."

Emily shined the flashlight around, looking for one she had seen down here when she first entered. She found it behind the potato barrel. Turning it on, she gave it to Brandi and climbed the stairs into the barn. She saw Teddy sitting on his haunches in front of Mr. Riley, one hand still held the sweater to his head. Seeing her emerge from the stairwell, he stood up and walked toward her. "How is he?"

"He's going to be okay. He's eating your brownie right now." She smiled wearily up at him and realized she was exhausted. Teddy put an arm around her and squeezed.

"Ouch!" she gasped.

"What's wrong?" he said releasing her.

"It's okay, sore rib." She glared at Frank Riley. "I'll live." She stepped back into the hug.

It felt wonderful until she realized he was shaking. Studying him more closely, she saw he was covered in dried blood.

"Are you okay? You look like something out of a slasher film."

Teddy removed the sweater to see if the blood flow was stopping. "He rammed me into one of the supports and I smacked my head."

"I know," she said, "I was the thing he used to ram you!"

Emily looked out of the barn and saw the sheriff's car heading up the road to the driveway, "Well, here comes Terd-berg." She smiled at her own joke. "And boy, am I glad to see him!"

The sheriff got out of his patrol car, his right hand resting on his gun. He surveyed the situation as he entered.

"You two mind telling me what's going on in here?" Then, noticing Teddy's appearance, he added, "You're the Johnson kid, aren't you?"

"Yes sir," answered Teddy.

"Do I need to call you an ambulance?"

"No sir," said Teddy, "I'll be fine."

The sheriff turned to Emily, "And you're a Jensen, right? I was out to your house last summer over that mess."

"Yes, Sheriff, and we'd be glad to tell you what happened, but first, there's a little boy named Michael handcuffed in the cellar. This guy abducted him. Our friend Brandi is with him, but I'm sure he'd like to get out of there if you have any keys we could use."

The sheriff looked at the man propped against the wall. "Riley, is that true?"

Mr. Riley looked up at the sheriff, tears in his eyes. "The key is in my shirt pocket, Sheriff."

Sheriff Terberg went back to his car and spoke on the radio for a minute, then came back into the barn, leaned forward and pulled a small key out of Mr. Riley's front pocket. "I'm gonna have to cuff you Frank."

He took handcuffs off his belt and snapped them onto Frank's hands, untying the jumper cables and handing them to Teddy. "You two seem to have this under control, mind if I have a look-see?"

Emily offered the small flashlight to the Sheriff who smiled, patting the huge one on his belt as he turned toward the root cellar. Teddy bent to sit against the barn next to Mr. Riley; Emily joined him. She couldn't remember ever feeling this tired. They rested there, trying to hear what was being said in the root cellar. Soon they heard steps coming up from below. Sheriff Terberg was carrying Michael who was still holding Brandi's hand. They were squinting against the relative light of the barn.

The sheriff sat Michael down on the barn floor, but Michael instantly flung himself into Brandi's arms. Terberg scratched his head as if trying to decide what to do.

"Here's the thing," he drawled, "Michael's mom already called the station when he didn't come home from school. I told dispatch to have her meet us at the station. I need the three of you and Michael to come in and make a statement and get you checked out for injuries. I also want to get Michael to his mom as soon as possible. But, I have to bring Riley in and my deputy's over at the Quincy jail." He looked out at the gathering snow. "I don't fancy waitin' for him to get here. The thing is, I think Michael will feel safer riding with you kids, is that okay?"

"Of course," agreed Brandi for them all.

"All right, Frank, it's time to go." The sheriff pulled Frank Riley to his feet and headed him toward his squad car.

Three weary warriors and a little boy followed behind.

CHAPTER TWENTY-TWO
SAMMY

SAMMY AND DAWNA ARRIVED at Denny's after the rest of the Blue Group was seated at their table. Lando saved Sammy a place next to him in the booth and as she slid into it he draped his arm around her shoulders. She felt slightly embarrassed as Tiff raised her eyebrows at Ty and he grinned knowingly.

"Well," said Ty, "It seems you have more to tell us than the news about the boy."

Sammy felt her checks getting pink, but Lando came to her rescue, "You might as well know that Sammy and I are dating." He grinned from ear to ear.

Tiff looked at Sammy in surprise, "When did this happen? Why didn't you tell me?"

Again Lando intervened, "It happened last weekend, when we went to Dawna's for Thanksgiving. And we wanted to tell you all at the same time, so I made Sammy promise not to tell, *or* change her Facebook status until our lunch."

"Well, that's great," said Tiff, "I'm really happy for you. So, what happened while you were in Sierraville to bring this about? Dawna, have you been playing matchmaker or something?"

"Not me," she held up her hands in protest. "They worked it out all on their own."

Lando beamed, "Sammy's going with me to my homecoming dance next month!"

Sammy was hoping Lando wouldn't bring that up just yet. It had been over a homecoming dance that Tiff and Ty ended their 'almost' relationship. She looked at Tiff to see how she was taking this news. She could see that, although still hurting, Tiff was trying to be supportive.

"We'll have to go shopping together to find you a dress," she said.

"That would be great, Tiff," Sammy beamed.

"Okay," Ty teasingly grumbled, "Enough about the lovebirds, I wanna hear about the boy in the barn. On the phone you said how they found him, but what happened next? How did they explain to the police *how* they found him?"

"I think Dawna should tell that part of the story," said Sammy.

Just then a waitress interrupted their discussion to take their orders. It didn't take long because they'd been coming here one Sunday a month since August and had the menu memorized.

"Well," Dawna teased to get everyone's attention after the waitress left, "they told the sheriff they were just coming home from school when they saw a man pick up a little boy in the snow. On a whim they followed him and when he pulled up at a derelict barn they decided to call for help."

"That's it?" asked Tiff.

"That's it," said Dawna. "And get this, it turns out the guy had already been convicted as a pedophile in California. He's a tier 3 sex offender! So, he's probably going to jail for a long time. I'm so glad they got there when they did."

"Me too," said Tiff. "So what's happening to Emily now, and the others?"

Dawna grinned, "The town has practically sainted the three of them, and they're like local heroes." She looked down at her lap. When she glanced up again she had tears in her eyes.

Sammy felt her body tighten, somehow knowing she wouldn't like whatever Dawna was about to say.

"…and, the three of them decided to launch this campaign to bring me back to Sierraville."

Sammy sucked in her breath in surprise. "What? What do you mean?"

Dawna's eyes pleaded. Sammy knew Dawna wanted to go home. They both knew how hard it would be on Sammy if she left.

Dawna continued, "They want me to come home and finish out my junior and senior year in Sierraville, to graduate from my own school." She looked at Sammy, begging silently for understanding.

Sammy felt Lando's arm tighten around her and took a deep breath. She had never had a best friend before. Tiff was the closest thing before Dawna came along and going to different schools made their friendship difficult. But, she wasn't alone in the world anymore, either. She had Lando, Tiff and Ty. She had the tech team from the drama department. Suddenly she realized Dawna was waiting for her to say something.

"In a way, I think you should go back."

"Really! You do?"

"Yeah, of course, you deserve to graduate with your friends. And, you should be with your family."

Dawna practically jumped over the table to hug Sammy. When she pulled away, both girls' faces were wet with tears. Tiff's beautiful eyes glistened too.

Dawna continued, "I promise I'll call, and text and Facebook. And I promise to come back for the play."

"You'd better, you made the costumes." Sammy took a deep breath, "Boy, am I gonna miss you."

EPILOGUE
THE RALLY
SIERRAVILLE, CALIFORNIA, DECEMBER 19TH

EMILY COULDN'T BELIEVE IT. She was actually standing in front of her entire school at a pep rally. She and Teddy were standing center stage next to Brandi Burgess. The principal, Mrs. Rountree, was telling the entire school what good citizens and role models they were. Even though until three weeks ago, she probably didn't know Emily's name. Emily felt her heart thudding in her chest and prayed the principal wouldn't ask her to say anything. She couldn't have gotten out a coherent sentence if she'd tried. Teddy looked as stunned as she felt. If they had to stand up here much longer, he'd pass right out. Taking his hand, she gave it a quick squeeze. He looked at her and smiled the most beautiful smile Emily had ever seen. Had he always had such pretty eyes?

Michael Canfield, the little boy they'd rescued, came forward with his mother to present the three of them with bouquets of roses. He looked a lot better than the last time Emily saw him, rubbing his wrist after the sheriff unlocked the handcuffs, then jumping into his mother's arms at the station. Now his mother was hugging each of them and crying as Michael passed out the flowers.

Emily scanned the crowd. Her family, Teddy's parents and Brandi's parents all sat together in the stands to her left. She glanced up at her parents who were beaming, and then she relaxed. Dawna sat next to her mom. Her sister was finally home! Emily had not seen her come in and she needed to be here today. This was her day, even more than Emily's. They grinned at each other and Dawna gave her a thumbs-up.

Finally, Mrs. Rountree handed the microphone to Brandi. Unlike Emily and Teddy, Brandi was in her element holding a microphone.

"Hello Grizzlies!" she shouted. The auditorium erupted in cheers. Brandi smiled her beautiful smile and waited for the roar to subside. Emily scanned the crowd. Every person in the gym was wearing a yellow ribbon that had been part of their "Bring Dawna Home" campaign. Banners reading "Bring Dawna Home" ringed the room. Emily wondered what Dawna thought about all of this. She looked at her and could tell she was overwhelmed.

Brandi continued, "Grizzles, two tragedies have touched our small community this year. We have learned some hard realities about the existence of sexual slavery and child abuse. I want you to turn around now and look at the people around you."

She waited until people realized she was serious. There was shuffling as the students and faculty looked around tentatively at each other.

"Statistically, one in every four girls and one in every six guys in this room have been sexually abused or will be by the time they're eighteen."

Emily looked out in the crowd and saw the now somber faces of her classmates. Who knew the assembly would take such a serious turn? She felt proud to be standing next to Brandi today.

Brandi continued, "This is something we need to come together as a community and fight against. You all know that our Family Resource Center is offering free counseling to anyone who needs to talk about these things. Please, please don't try to deal with this on your own, tell somebody. And if that person won't help you, tell again and again until someone does."

She paused, looking up to where Dawna sat, the eyes of the crowd following hers. "Our town has made some mistakes about how we've handled Dawna's kidnapping. We did not treat her or her family fairly. Let's not make the same mistakes with Michael and his mother." She looked over her shoulder and smiled at them. "We now know it is never, ever right to blame the victim. We have learned that when we turn against each other we crumble, but when we work together," at this she glanced over at Emily and Teddy, "we are strong enough to fight anything! We are Grizzly strong!" she yelled, pumping her fist into the air.

The crowd went crazy at this statement. Students started stomping their feet and chanting, "Grizzlies, Grizzlies, Grizzles!"

Brandi held up her hand and the room quieted again. "I'd like to ask Dawna Jensen to come down here please." Deafening cheers erupted as Dawna made her way slowly down the stands and onto the floor. Emily pulled Dawna to stand between her and Brandi.

"Dawna, on behalf of our school and our community, I want to apologize for the way we treated you. We hope that someday you and your family will be able to forgive us, and we want to ask you one question." The crowd collectively held its breath.

"Will you come home?"

The chant started immediately, "Come home! Come home! Come home!"

Dawna's eyes filled with tears as she looked around the room at her friends and teachers. Brandi held the microphone out toward her and the crowd grew silent. Dawna leaned into the microphone and said only two words. But they were the best words Emily had heard in her entire life.

"I will."

ACKNOWLEDGEMENTS

To my family, both by blood and adoption, who stand by me with love, pride and encouragement every day, and especially, my David, twenty-eight years and still my best friend. I love you all!

To the village who helped me whip this manuscript into shape: Kay Swindle, Derryl Baker, Ken Beaton and Barbara Jean from the Unnamed Writers group of Reno – you're the best!

To my editor Julie Ricks and friends at Lucky Bat Books—thank you, thank you!

To Bethany Spanier, my new sweeper, you rock!

To Chris Heifner for another great cover and book trailer; and Sarah Monahan for keeping the website awesome, love!

To a God who loves us all and longs for all to be loved, thank you!

DEAR READER

I HOPE YOU HAVE ENJOYED READING *The Bar* as much as I enjoyed writing it. If you'd like to talk about anything, drop me a line at www.JacciTurner.com.

If you need more information about sexual abuse or child abduction, please contact one of the resources listed below:

RAINN—Rape, Abuse, Incest National Network: www.rainn.org

Joyful Heart Foundation: www.joyfulheartfoundation.org

National Center for Missing or Exploited Children: www.missingkids.com

Much Love,

Jacci

13582442R00084

Made in the USA
Charleston, SC
19 July 2012